Rain DANCE

Tulsa
Thunderbirds

USA Today Bestselling Author
CATHERINE GAYLE

Dedication

This one is for all my readers who've ever been victims of domestic violence or abuse. You're not alone. And even if you're living in it now, know that there is help, but no one can help you if you don't help yourself. Please—help yourself. Find a way to get out.

Chapter One

Ethan

"You can't step on the lines, Dad," Carter said, rolling his eyes and putting a shit-ton of derision into the handful of words, as only a seven-year-old boy could do.

He wore a Thunderbirds sweater bearing my name and number. The sleeves were about three inches too long for him, but the length didn't matter since he'd rolled them up to above the elbow to combat the sweltering heat.

At the rate my son was shooting up, he'd outgrow this sweater and need the next size up before the season was over, anyway. He'd definitely taken after me in the size department. I hoped he wouldn't pass the six-foot mark before he was ten, but I had no intention of holding my breath.

I'd been almost six feet tall by the time I reached double digits in age. Too bad it'd taken until my late teens before the rest of my body had caught up.

Summer was lingering in Tulsa despite the fact that we were almost to mid-September already.

The entire state of Oklahoma was in the midst of a massive drought, even though fall typically brought a few thunderstorms. Not as many as we could expect in the spring, but hopefully enough to relieve the parched, dry earth.

I kept waiting for them to arrive, but so far…nothing. Not so much as a drop. The grass on my lawn was looking as brown and dry as straw lining a barn stall.

The lack of moisture only made everything about the heat seem hotter than ever.

"What happens if I step on the lines again?" I asked absentmindedly. I wasn't exactly thinking about following the rules of my son's game, especially since he tended to change them on a whim.

My thoughts were centered on the changes to our defensive system Tim Harvey, one of our assistant coaches, wanted us to institute for this upcoming season. Tonight had been the first time we'd employed it in a game situation, and it hadn't gone well.

At least we were still only in the preseason, though.

These games didn't count for anything that mattered. We just played them so we could learn the coaches' new systems and get our skating legs back under us after the long summer, and so the coaches and scouts could see how some of our prospects and the guys down at the AHL level were progressing in their development.

Carter let out an annoyed sigh. Apparently I wasn't very smart, at least in his esteemed opinion, since I couldn't keep up with his rules.

"The fire-breathing dragon comes up out of the ground and blasts you into next year," he said, his matter-of-fact tone further emphasizing my obvious idiocy. Clearly, based on his tone, I knew nothing about fire-breathing dragons, let alone the workings of a seven-year-old boy's mind.

Never mind the fact that I'd once been one, myself. A little boy, not a dragon. I'd only wished I were a dragon, because then I could have breathed fire all over my son-of-a-bitch father and saved both my mother and myself a hell of a lot of pain—both literally and figuratively.

Too bad dragons didn't exist in the real world, but only in the overactive imaginations of little boys. Either way, I intended to make damn sure that Carter never needed a dragon or anyone else to rescue him. He'd never find himself in a dangerous situation that he wasn't fully prepared to face. Not if I had anything to say about it.

"Maybe I want to step on the lines and bring out the dragon," I replied, intentionally egging him on.

"Only if you want to die."

"I don't know. I bet I could train a dragon and fly on it."

"Real dragons aren't like cartoon dragons, Dad." This time, the eye roll was only evident in Carter's tone, because he was too focused on the lines painted on the pavement to bother with craning his neck up far enough to look at me.

"I thought Toothless was real," I said in faux horror.

My son didn't worry about answering. He was too busy jumping over the white-and-yellow parking lines outside the BOK Center, because he was scared of dragons but not of me.

Which, frankly, was how it should be, whether

dragons were real or not. No kid should be scared of their father.

That was the one thing I'd promised myself when I'd married his mother and again when Carter was born—no matter what, my wife and child would never live in fear.

I wouldn't turn out to be like my father.

I was not a monster.

Maybe things hadn't worked out between Kinsey and me, but it wasn't because of violence. We just hadn't been suited to one another. Lots of marriages failed, for any number of reasons. Kinsey and I were still friends, though, and we worked together to make sure Carter would always know he was loved.

My kid would never fear me. That couldn't happen. It *wouldn't* happen. There were plenty of other things in this world that could scare him. I hoped he would grow up without fear, even if I knew that wasn't realistic. No one was completely without fear. But at least I could ensure it wasn't me who scared him.

A car came around the corner, going too fast, and I instinctively reached out one of my long arms and tugged my son back against me. Turned out it wasn't necessary. The driver must have seen us and swerved out of the way at the last second.

"Daaa-aaad," Carter complained. "You made me step on the line."

"Sorry for keeping you alive, kid. I'll let you get run over next time, hmm? That sound better?" Because it very well might have happened.

"Just don't make me step on the lines."

I chuckled. "Got it."

I supposed Kinsey and I were doing a pretty okay

job with Carter if he was more scared of releasing a fire-breathing dragon from the cracks in the pavement than he was of me. Although, maybe we should try a bit harder to instill a fear of crazy drivers in him. He needed to be aware.

Since I didn't have a wife anymore, Carter typically sat with one of the other guys' wives or girlfriends when he was in town for my games. This time, he'd sat with Ravyn Nash, Drew's wife, a woman he constantly told me was "cool" because she was a tattoo artist. She'd drawn a tattoo of our dog, Snoopy, on his arm using markers during intermission tonight to keep him entertained. I had a feeling he wouldn't let me wash it off him for a week, but if we went swimming enough, the chlorine in the pools would probably take care of it before too much time had passed.

We turned the corner of the building to get to the lot where the players all parked. About half of my teammates had left ahead of me, and several others were still in the building, getting treatment for various injuries or meeting with one of the coaches to go over their performance in the game tonight and find out if they were sticking with the big club or being sent back to their developmental team.

The arena was virtually deserted at this point, other than a handful of workers who would be cleaning up until the wee hours of the morning following the mess the fans had left. That, more than anything, had to be why I was shocked to hear shouting up ahead.

"Stupid bitch! What'd you do with the fucking keys?"

And then there was the unmistakable sound of flesh striking flesh, followed by a sob that ripped my heart out because it could have come from my mother.

My insides clenched into an all-too-familiar knot.

I knew the voice.

Couldn't place it.

Couldn't think clearly.

But I wasn't a little boy anymore.

I was a grown-ass man.

And I'd made sure I was big enough and strong enough to fight back when my father decided to hit either me or my mother.

In the back of my mind, I knew this wasn't my parents, but honestly, it didn't matter who it was.

This couldn't happen. Not in front of me. Not if I could do something to stop it.

I couldn't *let* it happen.

I damned sure wasn't going to walk away when my kid was watching.

I hauled Carter into my arms because I could move faster carrying him than I could with him walking, and then I took off running.

"The lines!" he complained, still not catching on.

I ignored him. Someone was getting hurt.

When I came around the corner, I skidded to a stop, in shock.

Hayes "Haymaker" Lennon, our hotshot top-line left wing, was hauling his girlfriend, Natalie Turner, off the ground by her long, blond hair.

Mascara-soaked tears left track marks on her cheeks, one of them bearing an unmistakable red welt, the result of a blow, which would soon turn black and blue.

Briefly, her eyes met mine, then skittered away as if she wished she hadn't seen me at all. She didn't make a sound. Not so much as a peep, so eerily, unnervingly similar to the way I'd endured so many beatings before I'd decided to fight back.

When Lennon reared back his fist to strike again, she winced and squeezed her eyes closed, Carter squeaked in terror, and I lost my shit.

Chapter Two

Natalie

I heard the thud of flesh meeting flesh, the little boy's screams of terror, the shifting of gravel beneath bodies, the blaring of a car alarm going off, but I didn't feel the blow.

That was more of a shock to my system than anything else could have been.

Hayes still had a grip on my hair. He dragged me back down to the asphalt with him as he fell. My skull cracked against something, and I forced myself to stifle a sob. Crying only made it worse. Hayes always seemed to get off on my tears; I tried to never let him see how much he hurt me because then he would only hurt me worse.

Loose rock dug into my elbows, a sharp sensation that momentarily distracted me from the insistent throb in my head and the way my right eye was swelling shut.

"Dad!" the boy screamed, and then Hayes's grip on my hair relaxed.

The release happened so suddenly that my head

cracked back against the ground again, hard enough I wished I could black out.

Blacking out was always easier. But I wouldn't be so lucky tonight.

"You son of a bitch," Hayes spit out. But his voice was strained. Choked sounding, the way my voice did when he had a hand squeezing my windpipe. "Mind your own fucking business."

"It is my business if you're beating up a woman in front of my kid."

"Fuck you," Hayes shot back. "Take your kid home and worry about yourself."

I blinked until everything came into focus. But I could only see out of my left eye. The right one was already completely swollen shut.

Ethan Higgins, one of the other guys on the team, had a hand around Hayes's neck and was holding him down against the hood of a car. Ethan's son was standing nearby, fat tears silently pouring down his cheeks. They glistened in the streetlights in the parking lot, twinkling like the stars overhead.

No child should ever see this.

I needed to end it, for him if for no other reason.

I needed to end it for me, too.

Because the longer this went on, the worse it would be for me in the end. I knew that well enough by now.

My boyfriend was turning purple, but his wild eyes bored into me. This was all going to be my fault somehow. That was what he was trying to convey to me with that look, telling me my fate without bothering with words. His words were always hollow, anyway. The longer I allowed it to go on, the worse he would make me regret it.

"Please, stop," I said, but my words were barely more than a whisper, and Ethan didn't act as if he'd heard me at all. I cleared my throat, agonizingly pushed myself up from the ground, and tried again. Every nerve ending in my body screamed in pain, but pain and I were old friends these days. I could handle this. I forced a strength I didn't feel into my tone. "Let him go. Please."

My would-be rescuer didn't even glance in my direction, never taking his eyes from Hayes. "Carter, I need you to be a big man for me," he said to his son, his voice somehow calm and in control. "I need you to come get the keys out of my pocket, then take Miss Natalie and go get in the car with her. Got it?"

"She's not getting in your fucking car," Hayes spit out, kicking wildly and making contact with Ethan's shins, but the larger man didn't even flinch.

I knew how much that hurt. I knew how much power Hayes could put into a kick like that. I'd felt those kicks all over my body more times than I could count. He especially liked kicking my ribs when I was curled in the fetal position.

In fact, I felt those kicks now in commiseration with Ethan's plight. My entire body curled in on itself. In panic. In fear. In preparation for the beating Hayes would give me once we were home again.

He'd hit me in front of people a few times before, but it was never anyone who would have bothered to step in like this—it typically only happened when his best friends were over, and they were all drunk and maybe high. Those guys would never step in to stop him. They only egged him on.

Sometimes, they would hit me, too. Hayes always seemed to like that. He would puff up like a rooster, his chest heaving with pride and excited breathing, while watching his best friends beat me up.

He'd never fucked me longer or harder than he had the night he, Alex, and Jason had taken turns, with two of them holding me down while the third had lashed my backside with a leather belt. That time he'd even stripped me first, because he'd wanted his friends to see the red welts rising on my pale skin.

Not that I'd ever had much say in the matter, if any. But I'd never gotten the impression that Hayes needed a reason to beat me, even if he typically gave me one just before he pummeled my body.

They were at the house tonight, actually. Waiting for us to get home. Probably already drunk or high, or maybe both.

The three of them had grown up together. They were practically inseparable. They did everything together, including beat up Hayes's girl. They'd never given me the impression that I'd been the first they'd done this with—it hadn't felt new—which made me wonder if they also had girlfriends that they all beat up, or how many other girlfriends Hayes had shared with them before me. I might have been the first, since we'd been together for so long. If there had been others, though, I was just the one he'd chosen to keep. Lucky me. The only thing he hadn't allowed them to do was fuck me.

Yet.

He'd threatened it a few times, usually if I was still crying while he fucked me raw following a particularly brutal beating. *They get so fucking hard, like I do, watching you cry*, he'd tell me. *It's not fair to leave them to jerk off on their own. They could both fuck you at the same time, one in your ass, one in your pussy. It's only fair, you know.*

I wasn't sure if he just enjoyed seeing my panic at the thought of his best friends invading my body in that way or if he truly intended to let them do it one of these days.

Was tonight the night?

Whether he intended for that to happen or not, I knew what was waiting for me: a beating I'd never be able to forget, and maybe more. And the longer I put it off, the longer I allowed Ethan Higgins and his son to delay the inevitable, the worse Hayes's retribution would be.

Would tonight be the night he lost control and killed me? That might be a blessing in disguise.

"Come on, Carter," Ethan said, ignoring my boyfriend entirely—something I could never afford to do. "The keys are in my pants pocket. Right side in the front."

The little boy inched toward his father, sniffling but staring wide-eyed at the two men as he fished around in his father's pocket for the car keys. Once he had them, he walked over to me and held out a hand, looking solemn and serious and scared out of his wits. "Come on. Let's get in the car."

"You're not getting in his fucking car," Hayes choked out. His face was looking closer to blue than red now.

Was that how I looked when he choked me? Did my skin take on that purplish tinge?

"No," I said, somehow calm despite the fear-laced adrenaline rushing through my body. "I'm not getting in his car."

Ethan stared at me so hard I thought I'd melt from the heat of his glare. "I'm not letting you go home with this son of a bitch."

"You can't stop her," Hayes bit off.

"I can call the cops. There might still be some on the property, actually. A few tend to stick around after games."

"And I can have you arrested for assault when they show up," he shot back. "Want your kid to see that?"

"They'd arrest you, too," Ethan said.

"Only if she presses charges, which she won't do. Either way, your kid sees you being hauled off to jail. Good plan, hero. What a fucking dad."

I could feel the heat of both men's stares boring into me, one daring me to contradict him, the other begging me to do exactly that.

And there was the crux of the problem. Hayes knew I wouldn't press charges. He knew he never had to worry about that.

Because I had nowhere else to go. No one else to turn to.

He'd made sure of that a long time ago.

But why did Ethan care? What was in it for him? I couldn't wrap my brain around it.

Carter urgently tugged on my hand again. "Come on. Let's get in the car like Dad said. I'll help you."

I allowed him to tug me to my feet, but then I broke free of his grip and crossed over to the two men. "Let him go," I pleaded, refusing to look into either man's eyes. I didn't want to feel the anger in Hayes's gaze or see the pity in Ethan's. "Please, just let him go and take your son home. He shouldn't see this."

But Ethan didn't release his grip on Hayes. If anything, he tightened it.

I might not be able to see Ethan's expression, but I could feel it boring into me. Pity? Disgust? Anger? I couldn't be sure.

"I need him to see this," Ethan said, but that response made no sense at all. "And I need you to get in my car." He was so solemn, as if there weren't any other possible response he could have.

"You know I can't do that," I whispered, silently pleading with him to understand. But why should I expect anyone else to understand when I couldn't wrap my mind around it, myself?

"I know you're scared to do that," he replied. "To get in my car. To trust someone. To try to get away from him. But going home with this piece of shit will be worse, and you know it."

How could I know that? With Hayes, at least I knew what to expect. I knew what I was getting into. If I did what Ethan asked of me, if I got into his car, then what?

It was the unknown. He was bigger and clearly stronger, so couldn't he do even more damage? Better the devil you know, right?

But then I made the mistake of looking up.

Hayes was glaring at me like he'd been possessed by a demon, his face red and wild and his eyes almost fully black, bulging out of the sockets with the sort of fury he typically only unleashed when we were at home. I wasn't entirely sure he *wasn't* a demon, to be honest. But there was nothing but kindness and empathy staring back at me in Ethan's expression.

It would be tempting to trust him. Tempting to believe in kindness.

I knew better than that, though. Kindness was nothing but a façade and trust had no place in my vocabulary.

"Please," I repeated, not allowing my gaze to

waver as I stared into eyes that looked black as night. "Just let him go. It's better this way."

"How is letting you go home with a monster better?" he replied, his grip seeming to tighten even more on Hayes's windpipe. "How is teaching my kid it's okay to walk away from someone in need *better*? Better than what?"

I couldn't answer his questions. There *was* no answer.

At least none that he would accept.

Hayes scrabbled to break Ethan's grip on his neck, kicking and flailing to get free as he could no longer speak due to lack of oxygen.

"You have to let him go," I pleaded. "If he dies, if you kill him, what'll that teach your son? You can't kill him." It was the only argument I had, the only one I could make. If he didn't go for it…

Apparently, it was the only argument that held any weight with Ethan. Thank goodness for that.

With a disgusted look, he threw Hayes back, releasing him with such force that my boyfriend skidded across the pavement and the car keys he had claimed I'd lost skittered out of his pants pocket, only coming to a stop when they collided with my feet.

Hayes coughed and spluttered, his hands pawing at his own neck in a similar manner to the ways I'd done when he'd encircled my throat with his punishing grip several times before. He would have bruises there, green, yellow, purple, nasty bruises where the redness remained. I should know. I'd borne them numerous times. That was why I wore so many turtlenecks, despite the sweltering Tulsa heat.

Ethan's eyes bored into me. I could feel the intensity of his gaze even though I refused to meet it.

He stalked over to his vehicle and ripped open the door, and I could finally take a breath—because he was leaving. This part of my torment was ending, and then I'd be left with Hayes and however he intended to make me pay for it.

But instead of climbing inside and starting the engine, Ethan rummaged in the center console for a moment. When he returned, it was with a bright turquoise Post-It note bearing the Thunderbirds logo, a phone number and address scrawled across it, penned by a hurried hand.

He passed it over to me, firmly closing my fingers around the scrap of paper. "Call me when you change your mind." Then he took his son's hand and led him to the car, making sure the crying boy was securely buckled into his booster seat in the back before driving away.

But long after he was gone, I could still feel the weight of Ethan's gaze on me. Begging me to come with him. Pleading. Imploring me.

I shoved the wadded-up note into my pocket next to my cell phone and tried to swallow past the lump in my throat as Hayes slowly dragged himself up off the ground, but it refused to budge. Regardless of the fact that I was doing what he wanted of me, this would all be my fault. I would pay once we were home. I knew it, and he knew it, and there was no getting around it.

"Get in the fucking car," he bit off, his voice harsher, raspier than normal, punching the button on the clicker until the parking lights flashed.

Without making a peep, I got into the passenger seat, closed the door, and fastened my seat belt, watching in the rearview mirror as Ethan's taillights faded in the distance, along with any hope I might have once had.

Hope was nothing but a lie.

Chapter Three

Ethan

"Why did he hit her, Dad?"

Carter was in his Snoopy pj's, snuggled up in his Snoopy sheets and blankets, with Snoopy—our yellow Labrador puppy, who was almost as big as Carter, even though both of them were still growing like weeds—curled up at his feet.

I brushed my son's hair out of his eyes and wished I had an answer. He had my hair and eyes, both dark brown. This was the hardest part of being a parent—trying to explain all the shit in the world when there wasn't a good explanation. "I don't know," I finally said. "You understand why I hit him, though, right?"

He sniffled and nodded, wide-eyed. "Because he was hurting Miss Natalie."

"And it's not right for a man to ever hit a woman or a child. We don't hit anyone."

"'Cept in hockey games sometimes," Carter said, repeating my explanation almost verbatim.

"That's right. Except in hockey games sometimes. But that's part of the rules, and it has consequences.

When you fight in a hockey game, you have to go to the penalty box."

Even though I had made sure he understood that fighting was an accepted part of the game I played, he'd never once seen me drop my gloves and fight on the ice. Fighting wasn't something I enjoyed. Besides, I could help my team better if I was on the ice than I could sitting in the box.

I'd hoped my son would never see me do it in any context. If he had to see it, though, I was glad it was because I was defending someone who couldn't defend herself. Because I was trying to right a wrong. Because it was the only thing I *could* do, given the circumstances.

"Is he going to hurt her again?" Carter asked, sniffling.

I took a tissue from the box on the nightstand and held it so he could blow his nose. "I don't know, Carter," I said cautiously, weighing each word before I let it leave my lips. "I hope not. I hope he won't hit her again."

That wasn't quite the truth, though. Yeah, I hoped he wouldn't beat her up when they got home, but I knew he would. Been there, done that. I'd recognized the haunted look in Natalie's pale-blue eyes. I'd seen the same quiet desperation in them that I'd seen in my own eyes for years. In my mother's eyes, too. The certainty that it wasn't over. The knowledge that she was bound to experience something even worse once they were alone.

He was probably beating the shit out of her right this very moment, a thought that made me physically ill.

I should've hauled her into my car, by force if

necessary. I should've called the cops. I should've done something—anything—other than walk away.

What the fuck kind of example was I setting for Carter?

The thought of what Natalie was probably going through right now had my stomach roiling. Because I knew. I fucking *knew* what was happening, and I hadn't managed to stop it. I'd tried, but trying wasn't good enough.

There had to be something else I could've done. Some scenario I hadn't contemplated, some argument I could've made. But nothing came to me, not even now, after the heat of the moment had died off and I could think clearly.

If she wasn't ready to get away, there wasn't anything I could do to change that.

Short of kidnapping her and rescuing her against her will, at least. And then would I be any better than Hayes?

It'd depend on how you looked at the situation, I supposed. I knew how *I* saw it, but how would *she* interpret something like that?

Carter patted the back of my hand consolingly, as if a simple touch could erase the memory of what he'd just witnessed. As if his touch could cleanse and purify my hands after they'd touched that pathetic excuse for a human being. Carter could almost do it, too. "She'll be okay, Dad."

"Yeah," I said, because he needed to hear it, not because I believed it.

"You'll take care of her."

But how could I take care of her if she wouldn't let me?

I finished reading Carter his bedtime story, then

gave both him and Snoopy kisses on their foreheads before turning out the light.

"Leave the door cracked tonight," Carter pleaded as I made my way out of his room.

He hadn't asked for that in a couple of years. Not since his nightmares had stopped.

Back in the early days, after Kinsey and I had split up, he'd had a lot of nightmares. Kids took everything in, thought it was all their fault. I knew that. I'd lived through that. So he'd blamed himself, somehow, for our inability to make our marriage work out, and it had manifested in nightmares.

But once we'd been able to convince him that Kinsey and I were still friends, and that we both still cared about each other and—most importantly—still loved him, the nightmares had come to an end. If they came back now, because of Hayes Fucking Lennon, that would give me one more reason to want the bastard dead.

I left the door cracked and switched off the lights, then headed back downstairs for a beer. Once I was relatively assured that Carter would be able to drift off to sleep, with Snoopy standing guard, I took out my cell and tried to come up with what I could possibly say to Kinsey to explain what'd happened.

No matter how long I stared at my phone, though, nothing came to me. So I did the only thing I could do.

I called her, despite the late hour.

"What's wrong?" she demanded, sounding half asleep. "Is Carter okay? What happened?"

"Carter's going to be fine," I cut in before she could get too worked up.

"Going to be? Meaning he's not now?"

"We witnessed a guy beating up his girlfriend after the game tonight," I said. "One of my teammates," I added, almost as an afterthought even though that was the last thing it should've been.

"Oh, shit," Kinsey breathed into the phone.

That didn't even begin to cover it.

"What'd you do?" she asked.

Because she *knew*. She knew all about my abusive father. She knew how I felt about this shit.

She fucking knew.

"I almost killed him," I admitted.

"Shit."

"Had the bastard's throat in my hands. I could've done it, Kinsey. I could've choked the life out of him. I was so close. So fucking close to doing it."

"But you didn't." She said it as if she knew that, too.

"No."

But already, I was second-guessing myself. Already, I wished I could turn back the clock and have a do-over, because that bastard deserved to die. And because I had an idea of what was happening to Natalie right this very moment.

And because I felt like a piece of shit for allowing it to happen.

"And Carter saw all of this?" my ex asked cautiously.

"Every last bit of it."

"But you talked to him about it afterward, right?"

"Talking doesn't undo it."

"No," she said on a weighted sigh. "But it'll help him understand."

Could a kid ever understand the kind of thing my son had witnessed tonight? I'd never been able to process it. I'd never understood what had led my father to do the kinds of shit he'd done. Why no one had ever stepped in and put an end to it.

My teachers and coaches had to have known. I'd gone to school every day covered in bruises and scars that couldn't be explained away by simply stating, *He's a hockey player, and hockey's a rough game*, or *You know how kids are these days*.

No one, not once in my life, had ever tried to stop him.

And now I was no better than any of them. Because I'd walked away. When it was all said and done, I had walked away and left Natalie to deal with it on her own.

I was as bad as Hayes.

Maybe I'd never lifted a finger against her, but I hadn't stopped him from doing it, either. Hell, I might have made things worse for her.

"He asked me to leave the door open tonight," I said.

"He just needs some reassurance. That's all it is. He needs to know you're there."

Yeah, I was here, all right. I only hoped it wasn't me he feared.

The rage that had welled up inside me and spilled over was unlike anything he'd ever seen before. He'd witnessed me almost kill a man. And he'd seen me walk away from a woman in need. Those were two things I'd vowed to myself that he would never, ever see, but they'd both happened in the same night.

"Is Snoopy sleeping with him?" Kinsey asked.

"That dog sleeps on his bed even when he's with you."

"Then he'll be fine. He's got his puppy to protect

him, and he's got his daddy in the next room. He'll be fine."

I only wished I were as confident as she was.

Chapter Four

Natalie

Alex's and Jason's cars were both parked at the curb when Hayes pulled into the driveway. My heart plummeted at the sight, even though I'd already anticipated their presence. Maybe, somewhere deep inside, I'd managed to convince myself that they wouldn't be here.

No such luck.

Hayes didn't press the button for the garage door to open until we were sitting in the driveway, which only increased my anticipation and dread. He hadn't said a single word the whole way home. His silence caused my thoughts to swirl at an alarming pace. I'd come up with about a thousand different scenarios about what I might be up against, each of them equally terrifying.

He pulled into the garage and put the car in park, but he didn't shut off the ignition.

I stayed perfectly still, trying to avoid any movement that might draw his ire. But I couldn't stop my chest from rising and falling, rising and falling, rising and falling, at breakneck speed. The longer he made me wait, the worse it always was, because the anticipation allowed my imagination to run away with me.

When he finally moved, I flinched. But he'd only reached for the buttons at the side of his seat to move it away from the steering wheel and angle the seat back farther than it already was.

He slipped his hand into his pocket and took out his cell phone. I tried not to peek at the screen while he repeatedly punched the on-screen buttons, but I couldn't stop my eyes from veering over long enough to realize he was sending a message to his two best friends. Only moments after he sent it, the screen lit up with a response.

I felt like I might puke with trepidation over whatever they were discussing.

Finally, after a few more exchanges, Hayes locked his phone screen and slipped the whole thing back into his pocket. Then he undid his zipper and took out his cock. He stroked it a few times, but that wasn't strictly necessary. He was already hard.

He always got hard when he hit me.

"Suck me off," he demanded. "Unless you want me to drag you out into the front yard, bend you over the goddamned fire hydrant, and fuck your ass for the whole neighborhood to see. Suck it!"

I blinked a couple of times, but then I bent over and took his length into my mouth. Because I didn't doubt he'd do exactly what he'd threatened, if not worse.

I slid the pointed tip of my tongue along the underside of his cock, the way he liked, but apparently that wasn't going to be enough for him tonight. He put one hand at the base of my skull and pushed, forcing me to take so much that I gagged, but he didn't let up.

He slipped his other hand inside the waistband of my jeans and started finger fucking my ass. I hated anal, and he knew it. I especially hated it without lube, so he often chose to forgo anything that would make it easier for me to bear. That was just one more way he liked to punish me.

Two fingers. Then a third.

He pushed down on the base of my skull so hard that I choked and fought for air, even as he added a fourth finger, stretching me so wide it brought a fresh wave of tears to my eyes.

"Don't you fucking dare puke on me," he ground out.

I swallowed my bile, my tears, and his cockhead, willing myself to endure whatever he intended to put me through. I just had to get through it. Survive this and move on to whatever was next.

I'd been existing in survival mode for so long now I didn't know anything else, any other way of living.

He thrust his hips up to meet me, forcing more than I could handle into my mouth, laughing as I struggled.

Just when I was sure I couldn't take it anymore, he said, "Fuck, I need that ass." And then he dragged me up by the hair. "Take off your jeans. *Now!*" he added when I didn't respond fast enough.

I fumbled with the button and fly, my head throbbing and swimming as I tugged them off my hips. I kicked to get them off one leg, wincing when I made contact with the center console. They got stuck on my left leg, but Hayes didn't let that stop him. He grabbed me by my thighs, forced me to straddle him with the steering wheel pressing into my back, and shoved his cock into my ass.

I whimpered at the invasion that his fingers couldn't have fully prepared me for, but I knew better than to complain.

"Ride me, bitch," he commanded, and he forced his fingers—the ones he'd used to stretch me—into my mouth so I tasted myself on him.

He pressed those fingers into my throat until I gagged on them, and I did my best to bounce up and down, but every movement felt as if it was ripping me to shreds inside.

At least it didn't take him long this time.

When he got close, he put both his arms beneath mine, wrapping his hands up to grab hold of my shoulders so he could slam my body onto him repeatedly. A few punishing strokes later, I felt his completion filling me.

He held me like that for a long time, either oblivious to my tears or reveling in them, his softening cock still buried deep in my ass, his head resting against my breasts, the steering wheel digging into my back.

But then he shoved me onto the passenger seat, tucked his cock back inside his pants, zipped up, and tossed his head back against the seat rest with a beleaguered sigh.

"How long?" he demanded, not bothering to look at me.

How long? I couldn't follow his train of thought. What exactly was he asking me?

Nothing in the countless scenarios I'd been contemplating would explain this question.

Giving him the wrong answer was typically worse than giving no answer, so I bit my tongue and kept quiet, hoping that would be the case tonight.

Hayes slammed both hands on the steering wheel, and I flinched when the horn blared.

"How long, bitch?" he roared. "Answer me! How long have you been fucking Higgins behind my back?"

I was so taken aback by the question that I couldn't come up with an answer fast enough to appease him.

His right arm shot out quicker than I could blink, and he grabbed a fistful of my hair. "Fucking cheating bitch."

Then he was dragging me across the center console by my hair. My scalp was on fire. My knees hit hard on the concrete floor of the garage, scraping as he dragged me, and tears poured down my cheeks like a waterfall, but I couldn't even let out a squeak of pain or horror.

"You want to fuck around on me?" Hayes shouted, throwing open the door to the kitchen. He dragged me halfway through the house and threw me on the floor of the living room, then kicked me hard in the ribs, so hard all I could do was curl in on myself. "You want to make a fool out of me? You want to be a fucking whore, like Razor's girl, huh? You like fucking other men?"

His foot landed on the back of my skull, making me see stars. Then he kicked again, connecting with the small of my back. And again, right on the ribs.

Again and again and again, he kicked me until I was nothing but a sobbing ball of pain.

Some kicks landed on my face, and my other eye

swelled closed. My lip felt fat and I tasted blood. I wasn't sure when the other two guys had joined in, but they were there. Laughing. Egging one another on. Kicking me just as hard as Hayes was.

"She wants to be a whore, let's make her into a fucking whore," Hayes ground out.

Someone grabbed me by the hair and dragged me off the floor. Then they were ripping at what was left of my clothes, tearing them from my body, but they left my jeans dangling from a single ankle, and my mouth was forced down onto a hard cock until I choked and gagged on it, and another was splitting into my already sore and abused ass, and I felt like I was being ripped in two.

I'd never prayed before. But right now seemed like a good time to start. For the first time in my life, I said a silent prayer.

I prayed for it all to end.

Somehow.

Someway.

I didn't even care how.

I just needed it to end.

Death sounded like the best option, but I didn't get the impression Hayes would let me off so easily.

......

When I came to, I could only tell the sun was up because of the reddish glow behind my closed eyelids. I couldn't open one eye at all, although the other opened just a crack and seemed as if I might eventually be able to pry it all the way open if I worked at it diligently. They were both still swollen, painful and puffy and burning, just like the rest of me.

Even the cool sheets against my skin hurt when I tested my fingers to see if I could move them.

Huh. Sheets.

I didn't remember being put in the bed. Hayes must have brought me up here sometime after I'd passed out from sheer exhaustion.

I needed to pee, but the second I shifted my hips, I wished I hadn't. My entire body felt as if it were on fire. I couldn't stop myself from letting out a whimper. Hayes rolled over, causing the mattress to dip, and drew a hand over my cheek, then slid it down the column of my neck.

I froze, wondering if he would strangle me and end it once and for all, but I had no such luck.

He moved on, tracing the line of my collarbone, brushing over my breast, trailing down my belly, and then settling his hand at the aching, swollen apex of my thighs. He pinched my clit so hard I couldn't stop myself from whimpering in pain.

"See what happens when you fuck around on me, baby? You made me do this, you know. You got me so fucking jealous I couldn't stand it."

He leaned over me, forcing his tongue into my battered mouth. He pried my thighs apart, stretched one of my legs all the way up until my ankle was above my head, hefted his weight over me, and settled himself at my core.

The hard evidence of his arousal had me cringing in trepidation. Pussy or ass? Which would be worse right now? I honestly wasn't sure.

With a swift thrust, he impaled me, choosing my ass again, and I couldn't stop the moan of pain from falling through my lips. He crushed his hard, powerful body to me, lowered his head next to mine, and drove into me repeatedly. But at least he came quickly, grunting against my ear as he stilled, the warmth of his semen seeming to burn a hole inside me.

When he rolled off me, he brushed the hair back from my face. "I've gotta go to practice. Alex and Jason are going to stick around today, though. They'll take good care of you. You do whatever they tell you, baby, all right? They're resting up now, but they'll come take care of you after a bit."

In my present condition, I doubted I could do anything at all, and I *knew* Alex and Jason had no intention of doing anything that would remotely resemble *taking care of me*. They might beat me. They might rape me some more. They might do all of the above and then some.

The thought of being alone with them terrified me.

I mumbled something that Hayes seemed to accept as my acquiescence, because then he rolled out of bed. A moment later, I heard the shower running, followed by Hayes's tone-deaf singing to himself.

I curled in on myself, trying to find a comfortable position even though there was no such thing. My left leg didn't want to come with the rest of me, so I tugged harder and finally got it to budge.

Why was it being so difficult?

Had they broken some of my bones? Maybe. I honestly wasn't sure, because I couldn't move enough to test them out.

Had they ripped me open internally? Probably. Everything felt like fire down below. I dreaded trying to go to the bathroom even though I was practically bursting with the need to pee.

The shower cut off, and a few minutes later, Hayes was leaning over me again, kissing my swollen cheek. "Be a good girl, Nat. I don't like having to punish you."

Then, finally, blessedly, he was gone.

But at least his buddies didn't immediately come up the stairs to replace him.

I tugged once more on my left leg, and I realized that my jeans were still caught around my ankle. In all the frenzy of beating me and fucking me, they'd never fully removed them from my body.

In the distance, I heard the gentle hum of Hayes starting the car. Then it faded, and the rattling of the garage door closing behind him acted as a jumpstart to my survival instincts.

Hayes was gone.

Alex and Jason were still somewhere in the house, but they were sleeping, and not *here*, where they could hurt me.

The memory of a wadded-up sticky note flashed through my mind.

And then I thought of my cell phone, because I'd shoved the bit of paper into the pocket where I kept my phone. But even if it was still there, even if Hayes hadn't destroyed it or simply removed it while I was passed out, could I pry my eyes open far enough to do anything with it?

I heard the unmistakable sounds of movement from downstairs, which meant that Jason and Alex— or at least one of them—was stirring.

I didn't have much time.

I contorted my body as best I could, flinging my left leg up toward me so that the bulk of my jeans shifted toward my hands. My hands were swollen and painful, but I somehow forced one into my pocket. Nothing there, but I couldn't see to tell which pocket I'd started with. I shifted the material with my hands, bunching up the fabric so I could feel for something solid, and then, just as I heard the unmistakable grunt of one of the guys shuffling through the hall toward the downstairs bathroom, my fingers brushed over my phone.

Despite the pain, I somehow managed to close my hand around the phone and tug it free of my pocket.

The toilet flushed, which meant I might not have long at all before I had company. Seconds? Minutes, maybe, if I was lucky.

I lifted my other hand to my face and tried to pry the eyelid of my left eye open since it seemed to be in better shape than the right. It burned and stung, hot tears assaulting me to soothe the sting, but with my fingers, I managed to open it enough that I could just make out the numbers on the phone.

I couldn't risk speaking. The sound of my voice would draw the guys to the bedroom.

Should I call 9-1-1 and leave the line open, and then hope that the emergency operator could figure out that I needed help? But since it was a cell and not a landline, how would they be able to find me if I couldn't tell them an address? I wasn't sure how that worked.

I quickly nixed that idea. Too risky, and far too uncertain.

But…there was still the sticky note Ethan had given me with his phone number. Surely it had to be in that pocket. If they hadn't bothered to take my phone from me, there was no way they would have thought to do anything about a scrap of paper.

I contorted my body once again, tugging my leg toward my chest so I could dig through the pockets.

More feet shuffling in the hall. Muffled voices. They were both awake.

Panic had my chest heaving. My breathing turned slow, shallow, the oxygen rattling in my chest in an imitation of pneumonia.

Then I felt it, one finger brushing against the corner of the paper.

The toilet flushed again. *Fuck*.

I stretched my fingers as far as they would go. Finally managed to trap the paper between two fingers. Careful not to lose my grip on it, I tugged it free of my jeans and quickly flattened it out so I could read the numbers.

I opened a new message and punched in Ethan's digits as quickly as I could.

Deep, masculine voices rumbled in the hall, very close to the door, but my head was in a fog so I couldn't make out what they were saying.

I typed out the only thing I could think of. The only thing I had time for.

911 Nat—

The door opened before I could finish spelling out my name, so I hit *Send* and dropped the phone in the sheets, hoping they wouldn't notice. Hoping Ethan would understand. Hoping he would help me.

"Morning, sunshine," Alex said seconds before he and Jason sat on either side of me, their combined weight causing the mattress to dip. Alex reached for one of my hands and guided it to his cock, closing my fingers around his length and forcing me to stroke him to readiness. "What do you say about a nice wake-up fuck to start the day, hmm?"

He didn't really want an answer. I knew it, and they knew it. And even if he did, I couldn't answer because Jason had already straddled my chest and was shoving his hard dick between my battered, swollen lips.

I prayed that Ethan would see my text message and act on it. I clung to the desperate hope that he would help me, even though I knew it wouldn't happen.

No one could get me out of this.

Get through it. Endure it. *Survive*.

That was all I could think. It was all I could do.

Survival was the best I could hope for.

Although, at the moment, with Alex settling himself between my bruised thighs and Jason's cock bringing up bile in my mouth, I wasn't sure I wanted to survive anymore. Death seemed more appealing. Maybe Jason would manage to cut off my air supply completely and I could suffocate on his dick.

There was a thought. Something I could hope for and hang on to. A tiny bit of solace in the nightmare I was being forced to bear.

Hot tears stung my eyes and tracked down my cheeks, and I tried to take more of his cock into my throat than I could manage in the hope that it would kill me.

I didn't want to endure. I couldn't bear the thought that I might somehow survive.

I just wanted it all to end.

Chapter Five

Ethan

L ennon had one hell of a shiner at practice. I only wished I'd done more damage than I had. I couldn't help but notice that his hands were kind of swollen, too. I didn't remember doing anything to him that would have caused it, but maybe he'd hurt them while trying to remove my fingers from his throat. Served the bastard right if that was the reason for the damage. I hoped it was due to something I'd done to him and not due to something he'd done to Natalie after they'd gone home.

The coaches called him in after practice was over for a meeting, presumably to find out what the hell he'd been doing to get a black eye. He'd been known to party and get into bar fights while out on the town with his previous team, so no doubt they were doing damage control. The team's owners wouldn't be happy about this because the behavior of the guys on the team would reflect on them.

I wasn't worried that he'd tell them I was the one who'd caused it. He'd have to explain why I'd done it, and that was the last thing a son of a bitch like Lennon would want. Abusers liked to keep their abuse quiet.

The rest of the boys called him Haymaker. I had been, too.

That was before.

Now that I knew he threw haymakers at women just for the hell of it, for fun, for sport, or however the hell he thought of it, I wasn't inclined to call him anything but Dirtbag, Piece of Shit, or Toe Scum.

Even those seemed too good for him.

I showered and got dressed to head home after briefly stopping in to request a meeting with the coaches and the general manager. I still hadn't quite decided what I intended to ask of them—whether I wanted to be traded or if I would insist on Lennon being shipped out or something else—but I'd have time to think about it. My meeting couldn't be arranged for a couple more days.

Either way, I had no intention of remaining on a team with this motherfucker. One of us had to go, and I wasn't overly particular which one it was. I couldn't fight as part of a team alongside someone like him.

Carter had spent the morning with Tallie and Harper Fielding, our starting goaltender's wife and daughter. I'd promised I'd take him out for ice cream when I picked him up. We had a date for burgers and ice cream at Braum's this afternoon—not somewhere I normally ate, but whatever. Carter liked it, and I liked to make my kid happy, so we were going. At least their burgers were good, for fast food.

On the way out of the building, I turned on my cell phone so I could shoot Tallie a text that I was on my way. Once it powered up, I heard the familiar *ding* signaling a message. With any luck, that didn't mean Carter had been acting like a little shit today.

I tossed my gym bag into the trunk and got in the car to blast the AC before looking.

Then my heart stopped.

911 Nat showed up from an unfamiliar number.

It had to be from Natalie. And she'd sent it four fucking hours ago.

But Lennon, the scumbag, had been at practice, the same as I had been.

I didn't understand. Not at all.

Maybe he'd beat her up again this morning before leaving the house? Maybe she hoped I could get to her before he came home?

I didn't know.

I tapped out a quick reply: *U ok?* and sent it.

No response.

I forced myself to wait another minute or two.

Still nothing.

Fuck.

I slammed the car into reverse, backed out, and took off. I pressed and held the button for Siri. "Send a text message to Tallie Fielding," I said.

"Okay, composing a text message for Tallie Fielding," Siri replied. "What should it say?"

"Can you keep Carter for a while? Emergency situation came up."

Siri repeated the message back to me and then I had her send it. I didn't even bother with waiting for Tallie to respond. She wouldn't mind. I knew it. And even if she did, this was quite possibly a life-or-death situation. She'd understand once I had a chance to explain it to her.

My house was on the way to Lennon's place. I stopped, raced inside, unlocked the safe, grabbed my handgun, made sure it was loaded before I could second-guess myself, and jumped back into the car.

It seemed as if every light turned red on my way. I'd never been prone to road rage before, but I found myself blaring on my car horn and swerving to get around vehicles that wouldn't move the fuck out of my way.

Finally got there. Two cars were parked at the curb, neither of them Lennon's.

Slammed my car into park, left the engine running, and raced to the door.

Unlocked. Thank fuck for that.

I cocked the gun, threw open the door, and rushed inside.

No one in the living room, but it was a mess, clothes strewn everywhere and furniture disheveled.

And some blood on the floors and the couch.

It looked like a fucking crime scene. I'd seen shit like this before, back when I was a kid. I'd been on the receiving end of beatings that left messes like this—but the clothes being everywhere was something new.

It turned my stomach.

Motherfucker. I should've killed the bastard last night. Should've tossed Natalie over my shoulder and put her in the car even though she didn't want to go with me. Taking her home with me last night, protecting her against her will, would've been better than this.

Coming from upstairs, I heard a muffled moan along with the familiar, rhythmic thumping of a bed hitting the wall.

I flew up the stairs.

The sounds were coming from the bedroom at the end of the hall, the one with the door closed. I braced myself for whatever I might find in there, flung it open, and nearly lost my shit.

Natalie was covered in cuts and bruises, not to mention the two bastards who were raping her, one above and the other below. They didn't even look up when I came in, a tangle of grunts and limbs. Maybe they'd just expected me to be Lennon coming to join the party, so they didn't bother to stop their fun.

They had a phone set up on a goddamned tripod, filming everything they were doing.

Thinking fast, I grabbed the phone in my left hand and kept it trained on them, holding my gun steady in my right. "Get off her," I bit off.

"The fuck?" the one on the top of the pile said. He turned red, bleary, stoned eyes my way. The second he registered the gun, he jumped up and fled to the side of the room. "Jase, stop, man."

The other guy finally caught on and shimmied out from under Natalie's bruised and broken body, his hands in the air where I could see them.

They both had some blood on their bodies.

Her blood.

Goddamned motherfucking raping sons of bitches.

I ought to kill them both. My finger itched to squeeze the trigger.

But death was too good for them.

Natalie moaned again.

I couldn't tell if she was aware of what was going on around her. Couldn't spare the time to check her out more fully because I couldn't afford to lose focus on the two bastards who'd raped and beaten her bloody.

Besides, Lennon could show up any minute.

I was a big dude, and I had a gun, but I also had a battered woman to get out of there. With three of them against just one of me, I could easily be overpowered. I had to get Natalie out of there. I couldn't risk her safety.

"Down on the floor," I said to the raping bastards. "Hands behind your backs."

They complied, even though they kept up a litany of threats and curses, so I propped the camera back on the tripod, focused it on them, and grabbed a pair of jeans from the floor. It had a belt still looped around it, so I used the belt to secure the first guy's wrists behind him and the jeans to tie up the other guy. There were some dirty socks nearby, which I shoved into their mouths. It took every ounce of restraint I possessed not to kick the shit out of them, but no matter how much I wanted to kill them, no matter how much they deserved to die, I couldn't afford to do that right now.

Besides, with the cell phone video, I had plenty of evidence.

Once I was reasonably certain they were secure, I gingerly wrapped Natalie's broken body in a blanket and picked her up. She whimpered, and her eyes were swollen shut. She didn't have enough strength to hold on to me, her body limp in my arms. I only hoped I wasn't hurting her worse, but that couldn't be helped. I had to get her out of here.

"I've got you," I assured her. "It's Ethan. You're going to be safe now." I would make sure of it.

Since her rapists were tied up, I shifted my grip on Natalie so I could carry her over one shoulder, even though I knew it had to hurt her. Then I engaged the safety on my gun and shoved it into my pocket so I could grab the cell phone that had been recording everything on my way out. I wanted as much evidence as I could possibly get my hands on.

Natalie moaned again when I set her in the passenger seat of my car.

"I know it hurts. I'm so sorry," I said, gingerly fastening the seat belt around her. "It'll be better soon. It's all going to be better soon."

Because that son of a bitch would never lay another finger on her again. Not if I had anything to say about it.

Once I had her secured in my car, I rushed around to the driver's side and took off for the hospital, calling the police on the way.

Chapter Six

Natalie

Strange, beeping sounds surrounded me, making my head throb. Or maybe my head was already throbbing and the beeps only made it worse.

I tried to pry my eyes open, but I couldn't. The effort made me ache everywhere, even in places I didn't realize could hurt until that very moment. I couldn't stop the pained sob from tearing through me.

"Try to be still," said a familiar, deep voice. "Just breathe, okay?"

I yearned to do whatever the voice told me, but doing what I was told hadn't ever worked out too well for me.

I couldn't place the voice. I couldn't make sense of the beeping or why I couldn't move a muscle or why I couldn't speak or open my eyes or why I didn't know where I was.

A large hand came over the back of mine. Warm. Soothing. "You're safe now," he said.

I stilled. But I would never feel safe again.

There was no such thing. Safety was an illusion.

It was nothing but a lie.

I tried to tug my hand free, but I couldn't. I jerked and thrashed, and the machines started beeping out of control, and then there were more voices, hands holding me down, pushing me against the bed, and I knew it was happening all over again.

They were going to beat me and rape me, and they'd tied me up and were holding me down, and there was nothing I could do.

I screamed, but my scream strangled and died in my throat around something that had been forced down it. Didn't feel like a cock, but I didn't know what it was. I wanted it out.

Or if I couldn't get it out, I wanted to die. I wanted it all to end.

I scratched and clawed, trying to get away, but they put straps on my arms and legs and kept me trapped, and I couldn't move at all.

Then something warm flooded through my body.

Maybe this was it.

Maybe they were going to kill me, once and for all, and I'd be done with it.

Maybe it would finally be over.

I hoped they would kill me this time. I hoped I would die. I hoped this was the end, because I couldn't bear the thought of going through anything else.

That was the last thought that crossed my mind as I drifted off again, a fitful sleep overtaking me.

......

The next time I woke, I wondered if I was alone with all the beeping, whirring machines, because I didn't hear any voices, couldn't feel any hands on me.

Was this heaven?

Hell?

No, not hell. I'd already lived there. Even if I couldn't see, couldn't move, couldn't speak, it wasn't as bad as what I'd lived through.

My leg ached and I tried to shift it into a new position, but I couldn't. The effort hurt, and I let out a pained sound. Probably a mistake, because it would alert them that I was awake.

"Try to be still," a feminine voice said from somewhere nearby—close enough I could reach out and touch her if only I could move my arms.

I didn't want to be still, though. I wanted to get away. I *had* to get away, now, while Hayes and his friends weren't beating me.

This was my only chance.

I tugged at my restraints, jerking wildly to get free, but they wouldn't budge. I couldn't tell if it was because the restraints were so strong or if it was because I was so weak. I started crying, screaming in frustration, desperate to escape before they came back and started beating me some more, but it didn't do any good, and the woman at my side tried to hold me down instead of helping me escape.

I wanted to scream at her. I wanted to pound her with my fists, to kick and claw and bite my way out of here, but the scuffling sounds of rushing feet flooded into the room, and then more hands were on me, forcing me to lie there and take it, which was apparently all I could ever do, and the warmth seeped into my veins once again.

Black nothingness claimed me.

I liked the nothingness. If anything was going to

claim me, I wanted it to be this.

......

"Do you know where you are?" a woman asked. I didn't recognize her voice, and although my eyes could crack open just a smidge, it was too painful to try to focus on anything.

I pressed them closed against the blinding light, wincing away.

The light hurt.

Everything hurt.

I didn't want to feel anything, nothing at all, not ever again, but right now I could feel *everything*. Far too much of everything.

It was torture.

I wanted it to end. I wanted to die.

Why wouldn't they let me die?

Hayes had to be behind it. He was keeping me alive. He wasn't finished with me yet.

What would it take to be rid of him? To be free?

Probably death.

I really wanted to die.

Maybe I could use one of these beeping machines to kill myself. Maybe I could find a way to press some buttons, get too much of the drugs they kept pumping into me, overdose, and just drift away. Maybe I could rip out one of these tubes and stab myself in the heart with the needle. Would the drugs going straight into my heart kill me? It was worth a shot.

I tried to move my limbs, but nothing would budge.

How could I kill myself if they wouldn't let me?

I screamed in frustration, but my scream was nothing but a broken, hollow, aching sound, despite the fat tears burning my eyes and tracking down my cheeks to the pillow beneath my head.

"Try to speak, Natalie," someone else said. Another woman, but this time the voice was familiar. I recognized it but couldn't place it.

A hand gently pressed to one of mine and squeezed, and I realized I could move my fingers. Just my fingers. I bent and straightened them a few times, slowly testing them out.

"Let me go," I pleaded, but my voice was nothing but a harsh whisper that I couldn't even understand myself. The act of getting those few simple words out took all the strength I had. I'd been straining, trying to get up, but now all I could do was collapse back against the bed that was my prison.

"You're in the hospital," the familiar voice said. "You've been hurt really badly, but you're going to be okay. You're safe now."

That was a lie.

I wasn't going to be okay.

And there was no such thing as *safe*.

I strained against my bonds again, determined to free myself. I kicked and thrashed and screamed an eerily silent scream, and all the machines started beeping as wildly as I fought.

The feet rushed back into the room, and something warm flooded my veins, and I was out again.

......

"Try to stay calm," the familiar voice said again, the next time I drifted back into the land of the living.

I preferred to be in the land of the dead.

It was peaceful there.

And I didn't hurt when I was there.

But here, everything hurt, especially my heart.

"We know you're scared and you're in pain. Ethan's on his way. She's always calmer when he's here," she added, as if speaking to someone else.

I tried to open my eyes. They burned like fire, but I finally managed to crack one set of eyelids apart. My vision was fuzzy. Everything was too bright, but I made out two women sitting in the chairs next to me.

When I looked down at myself, I saw what seemed to be dozens of tubes connected to my arms. I was in a hospital bed. One of my legs was immobilized in a cast that stopped above my knee, and it was elevated above the bed. I shifted my hips, but that made my ribs scream in pain, so I tried to stay very, very still.

I glanced over at the women again.

They were familiar, despite my fuzzy vision. Vaguely familiar, at least.

One of them reached for my hand, and I fought the urge to cringe away from her. Jerky movements were my enemy now, every bit as much as Hayes and Alex and Jason were.

Her touch was gentle, though. She held my hand as if I were delicate and fragile.

Maybe she was right about that. Maybe I was delicate and fragile.

I certainly felt as if one wrong move would cause every bone in my body to shatter, if they hadn't already done so.

"Who are you?" I croaked, not recognizing my own voice.

"Dana Zellinger," the woman holding my hand said.

Dana. She was one of the wives from the team. No

wonder she was familiar but not overly so.

Hayes had never allowed me to spend much time with any of them. He preferred to keep me away from them. Alone. It was easier to beat me up if I was all alone. If I didn't have anyone else to turn to. If there weren't other people around to ask questions, to wonder why I was bruised or cut or whatever.

Hayes.

Panic grabbed my throat and threatened to strangle me, just as he had so many times. I couldn't breathe, and my eyes stung so badly I had to force them closed, even though that meant I was back in the dark.

"Calm down, Natalie," Dana said smoothly. "You're safe here. You're in the hospital. It's just me and Tallie in the room with you, okay?"

"No one's gonna hurt you in here, honey," the other woman said.

Tallie.

I felt her move around to the other side of the bed, and she took hold of my free hand, and they both kept uttering soothing words and gently stroking my arms and hands and face, but I couldn't take any of it in.

"Take a deep breath, Natalie," Dana said. "In through your nose. Out through your mouth. Come on. You can do it."

I forced myself to take big, deep breaths, and gradually the machines surrounding me stopped beeping so erratically.

"I want to go back to sleep," I forced out. But I didn't just want to sleep.

I wanted it to end.

To all be over.

To never have to see or hear or feel or think about Hayes again.

"They need you to be awake for a while now, hon," Tallie said.

Right. Because it was more fun to torture someone who was awake. What was the fun in beating or fucking a dead girl?

I knew Hayes was behind this. He had to be. Why else would they have me tied down so I couldn't move? He'd chained me to this bed, I knew he had. He was making sure I was healthy enough that he could take me home again and start all over from scratch.

I might not understand why Dana and Tallie were helping him, but I knew they were. He was behind this. That was why I couldn't move. He'd imprisoned me now, more than he ever had before.

For all I knew, the tubes shooting drugs into my veins were merely sedating me so it would be easier for Hayes to beat me and fuck me some more.

It wasn't over.

It would never be over.

I would never be free.

Not unless I somehow got away.

I screamed and thrashed again, ripping at the tubes with my battered, swollen hands as silent cries ripped my throat raw.

People in green scrubs rushed into my room, pushing Dana and Tallie out of the way, and held me down to shoot more drugs into my system.

Then it was black. It was nothing.

I was nothing.

The black nothingness was my only solace. The only thing I craved.

I clung to it as if my life depended on it.
Because it did.

Chapter Seven

Ethan

"She seemed to understand what was going on for a little while," Dana said when I walked into Natalie's hospital room for my night shift with her, a few days after the ordeal. "It felt like she recognized she was safe and we were trying to help her. But then one of the doctors came in to check on her, and she started freaking out again. They had to give her another dose of the antipsychotics to calm her down so she wouldn't try to rip out the breathing tube."

"And then she was back in la-la land," Tallie finished.

I looked down at Natalie's sleeping form. Even in her sleep, she seemed tortured. Her eyes were moving at a frantic pace behind her eyelids. Her brows kept drawing together. In fear? In pain? Maybe a combination of them both and Lord only knew what else.

"You two should get out of here," I said, dragging an uncomfortable, low-backed lavender armchair closer to Natalie's hospital bed and taking up my spot for my nightly vigil. I'd been sleeping upright in a chair by her bedside, standing guard over her lifeless form, close enough I could stroke the back of her hand or move the hair away from her eyes. Close enough that I'd recognize even the slightest change, so I could relay it to the nurses whenever they made their rounds.

The room smelled the same way every time I came in—a combination of antiseptic and the sweet, lemony soap they used to bathe her, all tinged around the edges with fear and just a hint of hope.

Too much fear; not enough hope.

At this point, the doctors were relatively certain that Natalie would survive. What sort of condition she'd be in when they woke her up remained a mystery. I intended to be with her when we found out, no matter if it was good news or bad news.

"Go get some rest," I added when my teammates' wives didn't immediately leave. "Your kids need you."

Dana scowled, but she didn't argue with me when I brought up the kids. Finally, she started gathering up her things. "Promise you'll get some sleep in the recliner, at least."

"I can't sleep in those recliners," I pointed out. "They're too small for either of you. How the hell am I supposed to fit my body in one of those things?"

"Well, you should see if they can bring a cot in here for you, at least," she countered, apparently conceding that point.

"I'll go ask at the nurses' station," Tallie put in.

"I don't need a cot," I argued, because I had no intention of sleeping, but Tallie had already darted out the door.

"You've got to get some rest," Dana said. "You won't be any use to her or anyone else if you're not taking care of yourself."

Rest? That wouldn't be happening any time soon. I felt as if I hadn't properly slept in a month. Certainly not in the days since I'd hauled Natalie's almost lifeless body away from that house.

Regardless, Tallie and one of the nurses came back with a cot, albeit one that wasn't anywhere near long enough to fit me comfortably, much like the recliners. Hospital furniture wasn't made with someone of my stature in mind. I stood six and a half feet tall in my stocking feet, and I weighed over two hundred thirty pounds. I might crush the hospital's cot if I tried to sleep on it.

Nevertheless, the nurses brought it in and set it up on the floor near Natalie's bed, along with a pillow and blanket, still leaving enough room for the doctors and nurses to do whatever they'd need to do for her if I was asleep.

Then Tallie and Dana headed home for the night.

I wouldn't be using it. I had no intention of sleeping while I was here, watching over Natalie.

Every time I managed to doze off, I wished I hadn't, because something would happen. Some small change in her color or breathing that I might miss, or else my subconscious would take me back to images of the way I'd found her, mixed in with memories from my own childhood and my father beating the shit out of me.

Better to stay awake.

I felt tortured, but not in the same way Natalie had been. My torture was all internalized, living fully inside my head and wreaking havoc on me.

Because I could have stopped this from happening.

I could have prevented it. I could have dragged her home with me that night, dragged her kicking and screaming if necessary, but at least she wouldn't be in this kind of shape now if I'd done that.

She would have been safe. She would have been *whole*.

But then again, Lennon and his buddies would have gotten off if I'd done that. They might have gotten away scot-free, no matter how many times they'd done this kind of thing to her in the past.

Lennon might still get off, actually—a thought that sickened me like none other since his involvement was the most atrocious. He was the one she'd been dating. The one who should have loved her and taken care of her. Who should've protected her from sick fucks like his friends and himself.

His buddies had been captured on the cell phone video I'd taken with me, but Lennon wasn't in a single frame. There weren't any other videos or photos on the phone that would incriminate him, even though everyone knew he wasn't just involved but was the worst monster of them all.

His DNA had been found on and inside Natalie's body along with the other two bastards' DNA when they'd done the rape kit, but since they'd been cohabiting for so long, that wasn't enough to nail him for his crimes.

It *could* have been consensual, theoretically, before the other guys had gotten involved.

At least, that was what the cops said Lennon's defense attorneys would argue, and there wasn't any way to *prove* he'd raped and supposedly beaten her.

Which was complete and total bullshit if you asked me.

How could anyone look at this woman and think any part of what she'd been through had been consensual? That she'd wanted what they'd done to her?

But they said they needed more proof.

The cops had taken Lennon in for questioning. But since his buddies hadn't ratted him out and Natalie was still too sick to tell anyone anything, they hadn't arrested him.

Soon, hopefully.

They kept telling me they were working on putting together a case against him, enough that they could get an arraignment.

Enough that it would hold up.

For now, he'd only gone in to answer their questions a few times.

That, at least, had been enough for the team to warrant suspending him indefinitely without pay, pending the results of an internal investigation into the matter. But they'd only done so after I'd taken up the case with the Jernigans, who owned the team.

Mr. Jernigan was the preacher at one of the biggest evangelical churches in the country, one that had a nationally syndicated television broadcast of their services.

I'd had to appeal to his wife, who had always been overly concerned with appearances, asking if she wanted their church members to know they were employing a rapist and an abuser. The woman had tried to institute a swear jar in our locker room, for fuck's sake, so I doubted she'd want to have a piece of shit of Lennon's caliber associated with their church, their team, their brand, their image.

That, finally, had done the job when nothing else had gotten through to them.

She'd gone to the coaching staff and the general manager and put her foot down, insisting that Lennon couldn't play again until and unless he was cleared of all wrongdoing involving Natalie.

Which wouldn't happen. It *couldn't* happen.

But a suspension still wasn't enough for me.

It was only temporary.

The shit he'd done to Natalie? That was permanent. I wanted the son of a bitch to rot in jail for all the shit he'd done to her.

So I'd made it known to everyone involved with the team that I wouldn't ever step out on the ice with the son of a bitch again.

Never.

Either he had to go or I did.

They could suspend my ass for refusing to play. Whatever. I didn't care.

But I wasn't suiting up and fighting alongside that bastard ever again. If I did, I'd probably kill him with my bare hands while an entire arena full of people watched, not to mention potentially millions of people looking on at home.

I doubted the aftermath of something like that would appeal to any of them.

Sure enough, once I'd laid down my ultimatum, they'd suspended Lennon and not me.

But the son of a bitch still hadn't been arrested.

I kept hoping the security cameras from the BOK Center would have caught some footage of Lennon beating the shit out of Natalie in the parking lot that night, but somehow not a single camera had captured it.

Don't ask me how that was possible, since they had cameras on almost every fucking lamp post, but none had recorded any footage of him. There was one where I could tell they were just out of the frame, because it showed me picking up Carter and rushing off the screen, but none of the others had been focused on us once I'd caught up to the bastard.

One of the cops had suggested that Lennon had planned it that way—he'd parked in an area where he'd known there wouldn't be any cameras on his car, and he'd waited until they were out of range before beginning his attack.

That only made it worse, in my mind, because it meant this hadn't been some random outburst. The assault hadn't been triggered by anything Natalie had done or failed to do; Lennon had been planning it all along. Having his buddies at the house and ready to join in only drove that point home further.

Regardless, he wasn't on any of the film, so proving his involvement was going to be tricky. Essentially, until Natalie woke up and was coherent enough to talk about it, everything that had gone down that night boiled down to it being my word against his.

The investigators had talked to Carter before I'd put him on a plane to go home to his mother. He'd told them what we'd seen in the parking lot, but the word of a seven-year-old boy apparently wouldn't hold much weight in court.

Bullshit if you asked me. I'd have been a hell of a witness against my father at that age, if anyone would have bothered to notice he was beating the shit out of me.

But no dice. They weren't going to involve Carter in things.

So now, we had to wait for Natalie to heal enough that she could talk about it.

And hope that she would.

Since she'd finally asked for help—albeit almost too late for me to do any good—I hoped she'd be ready to put the assholes responsible for her condition behind bars.

But first we needed her to wake up…and I had no idea what to expect once she did.

After Dana and Tallie had gathered up all of their things and left to go home for the night, I gingerly took Natalie's hand in mine, silently willing her to keep fighting.

The sons of bitches had broken her right eye socket, her nose, a couple of ribs, and her left leg. The broken ribs had punctured her spleen, which had necessitated the doctors opening her up and doing some internal repairs. And with all the facial fractures, she'd had a ton of swelling, which made it difficult for her to breathe, and they'd had to intubate her for a few days.

In her sleep, she'd kept trying to rip the tube out of her throat, so they'd put her on more medications to keep her calm, but those medications sometimes caused hallucinations, according to her nurses.

In short, there was no telling what she thought was happening to her.

Could it be worse than what she'd already been living through for God only knew how long? Maybe, although I couldn't imagine much being worse than the way I'd found her.

All I knew was that the doctors and nurses, and

especially the WAGs who'd been sitting with her during the times I couldn't be there, told me she was calmer when I was with her than when I wasn't.

I wished I could sit by her side all the time. I was damned sure going to sit here as much as I possibly could, because I needed her to be calm, to feel safe and secure and protected, so she could heal.

And I needed to be the one to protect her when it was all said and done. Not that I could explain why, exactly, other than the fact that I *knew* her.

Maybe I didn't know Natalie very well in some ways. I couldn't name her favorite movies or TV shows or musicians. I didn't know if she liked to read or swim or go nature hiking.

But I knew her better than she could possibly realize in other ways.

I knew the fear she'd been living in.

I knew she probably blamed herself, even if somewhere, deep inside, she knew that was bullshit and there was no one to blame but the sons of bitches who'd hurt her.

I knew she'd spend the rest of her life trying to get past it but that she never truly would—because this wasn't the sort of thing a person could ever just *get over.*

I knew she'd be lucky if she could come out of this and begin to live any semblance of a normal life.

I knew she might never trust another man again, let alone be brave enough to let someone love her, and that broke my heart for her. Because of a few assholes, she might spend her life pushing good men away.

She might push *me* away.

And if she did, I had to find the strength to allow

it, because I would *never*, not ever, force anything on any woman. And I especially wouldn't force myself upon her, not even if I knew having me in her life would be for the best.

So while I might not know her favorite color, I *knew* Natalie.

And my heart broke for her.

I wanted to help her.

I wanted her to know that, while some men were absolute pieces of shit, there were some good guys out there, too.

I wanted her to smile and laugh and live.

I wanted her to be free, but I knew enough to realize I might be asking for too much.

She might never be free.

But if I had anything to say about it, she'd have a chance. And that was more than a lot of people in her position would ever get.

If anyone should know and understand that, it was me. I'd fought for my chance.

Now I had to convince Natalie to fight for hers.

Chapter Eight

Natalie

Sometimes when I woke up, I was alone with the beeping machines and the awful fluorescent lighting and the voices paging doctors and nurses over the hospital's intercom system, unable to move a muscle or speak. I sometimes tried to speak, but I couldn't make much sound—barely more than a squeak—and no one was there to hear me anyway, even if I could have called out at the top of my lungs.

Other times, a nurse would be in the room with me, changing out the IV bag or checking my vital signs. "You're looking a lot better. You're getting your color back," they'd invariably say, but that only made me wonder, *better than what?* Because I felt like death, and not even the warmed-over variety. Or an orderly might say, "Why don't you try sitting up in the chair for a while? Or we could at least raise your bed to a sitting position. You're going to have to start moving around on your own soon, you know."

But I didn't know anything of the sort.

Dead people didn't move, as far as I was aware.

And wasn't I at least halfway to dead? I had to be. Except, every time they said something like that to me, I felt a little less dead than I had the time before, which frustrated me every bit as much as it gave them encouragement.

Then there were the times that I came to and small groupings of women and sometimes children surrounded me. They were familiar to me, even though I couldn't place them at first. But gradually their names started coming back to me, and I could match them up with their faces.

There was Dana Zellinger and her passel of kids and the understanding smile she always bore whenever she'd speak to me. She had a calming, soothing presence, even amidst the chaos that was now my life.

And then, there was Viktoriya Chambers, the ballerina who brought me delicate, homemade Russian desserts. "Svetka taught me," she'd say, her accent heavy, and she'd pass them out to the nurses, as well, because this Svetka, whoever that was, had also taught Viktoriya the importance of feeding everyone she came into contact with, and particularly those who were caring for others.

Ravyn Nash was unforgettable because of her head full of lavender dreadlocks as well as the bright tattoos covering her body. She spent most of her visits quietly sketching in a chair by the window, using pens and markers and pastels. Occasionally she asked if I needed anything, to which I could only shake my head. Sometimes, she would show me the sketches. One was a butterfly perched on a flower. Another was a stained-glass window with a naked woman stepping under a waterfall. They were tattoos she was designing for her clients, she told me. But there was one she wouldn't show me at all. I yearned to know what it was at the same time as I dreaded it—because she kept glancing over at me while she worked, and I was afraid she was drawing *me*.

London Nazarenko tended to sit next to my bed in her wheelchair, talking my ear off about how we were going to have races once they let me out of the bed and put me in a wheelchair of my own. The thought of wheelchair races only made me wonder if I would never be able to walk again. I tried wiggling my toes every time she talked about those things, and it *seemed* as if they all moved, but I couldn't see them to be sure. My left ankle wouldn't move at all, though. My knee wouldn't move either, actually. And since no one could understand anything I said—my voice was completely gone, and I didn't have any idea when it would return, if ever—worst of all, I couldn't ask anyone to explain it to me. She usually had her son with her, a toddler named Erik, who liked to eat the scrambled eggs they brought me every morning but I couldn't choke down. I was happy to let him have them.

But more often when I woke, Ethan Higgins was by my bed.

Somehow, I could breathe more freely when he was with me. I didn't feel strangled or suffocated. I didn't feel as if my pulse would slow to a crawl and then gradually die off; instead, it thumped strong enough I could count off every beat, almost so loud I could hear it.

With everyone else, I felt frustrated because I couldn't tell them what I needed to tell them. I got annoyed if they hovered too much, or if they didn't hover enough, and I could vacillate between the two in an instant because I couldn't *do* anything for myself, not even something as simple as opening the container of orange juice they brought daily with my breakfast, or wrangling my fork out of the plastic packaging surrounding my utensils and napkin.

But with Ethan in my hospital room, I didn't suffer the same frustrations.

He would fold his huge body into one of the too-small chairs in the room, which had to be horribly uncomfortable, and sit by my side.

Most of the time, he didn't say anything. I often opened my eyes after a nap and found him staring at me. Not in a creepy way, though. He stared as if trying to catalog everything about me.

When the nurses came in, he recited a long list of my vital signs and any tiny changes he might have observed in me, whether it was a rattle in my breathing, or the fact that my pulse slowed every time I drifted off to sleep and he wondered if that was normal or if they needed to do something about it, or even the tiny pink bump he'd noticed on the back of my hand that he wanted them to check out, in case it posed a concern.

How had he noticed the bump on my hand? I could barely even feel it if I dragged the pad of the thumb from my other hand across it, so why would he notice such a thing?

I was a mess of cuts, bruises, broken bones, and tubes running through my body until I couldn't tell where the machines ended and I began, but Ethan somehow saw everything.

He saw *me*.

It was enough to make me cry for wishing he were

with me during all the times he wasn't, while at the same time wishing he would stay away because I didn't want to be noticed.

Being noticed could only bring me danger. With Hayes, any time I'd somehow gone without him noticing me, I also went without him hitting me.

But Ethan's attention was different, somehow. He made me feel precious and cared for. I was terrified of getting too accustomed to the ways he made me feel, because it couldn't last. It was only a façade, something that would fade away with time, much like the cuts and bruises were already starting to fade.

I tried to guard myself against the loss of him, because it was coming. Nothing good in my life ever lasted. The only things that stuck around were the bad things, the ones I wanted to be free from, like Hayes.

Hayes. He hadn't been here, not once, at least not when I'd been awake. I wanted to ask about him, but I couldn't make anyone understand me.

Slowly but surely, my voice was growing stronger, but I still wasn't ready to ask this question. Because I didn't want to know the answer. I *feared* the answer.

Sometime soon, though, I'd have to ask. I wouldn't be able to put it off much longer.

If not for the small window on the other side of my room, I wouldn't know whether it was day or night. Everything ran together for me, with nurses coming in around the clock and waking me up in order to check my vital signs or change the bag of IV fluids or to give me another dose of some medication or another.

"You're starting to seem more like yourself," Dana Zellinger said to me one time.

More like myself? What did that mean? I shook my

head, confused.

"You seem like you're starting to understand what's going on," she said. "At first, every time you woke up, you were in another world, almost. We couldn't tell if you knew who we were or what was happening."

"I just want to go home," I said, almost sobbing the words, but at least they came out as something more than a whisper. But where was home? I didn't want to go back to Hayes. I didn't have anywhere to go. Not unless Hayes dragged me back once they let me leave the hospital. Would he do that? He might.

I couldn't go home with him. Not ever again. Not unless he was finally going to end it.

Dana's little boy patted her on the knee and said, "Up!" so she bent to pick him up and settle him on her lap.

"I don't know how soon they're going to let you leave," Dana said. "They're supposed to be moving you to the rehab unit later today, though, which is great news. It means you're that much closer to being allowed to go home."

And it also meant I was that much closer to having to figure out where I'd go and what I'd do with myself once I got there.

But still, no one mentioned Hayes.

I supposed I could try calling my parents and seeing if they would allow me to come back to their house. And what if they refused? When I'd first gotten involved with Hayes, they'd essentially cut me off. Besides, how would I get to Michigan in this kind of shape and with no money?

Thinking about these things only made my head hurt, so I decided not to focus on them too hard. I couldn't leave the hospital yet, anyway, so there was no point worrying about things I couldn't control.

Which, to be honest, was everything. I couldn't even control my bladder.

At some point, they'd taken out the catheter, but I was still receiving IV fluids and therefore needed to pee constantly. By the time I realized I needed to go, it was already too late, never mind the fact that I had to press my call button, wait for a nurse to arrive, which didn't always happen very soon, and gingerly make my way from the bed to the bathroom, which was awkward since I couldn't bend my left knee.

I started to wish they'd give me adult diapers, because that would be easier, even if I'd be mortified for anyone to see me that way.

But then again, how would being caught wearing diapers be worse than being seen in a puddle of my own urine? Or having everyone know all the things Hayes and his friends had done to me?

If I kept everything in perspective, the mortification level went down by a degree or so each time the nurses had to change my bedding.

Usually.

It depended entirely on who else happened to be in the room with me.

If it was one of the WAGs, I didn't mind too much. Especially not when it was London, because she followed it up by telling me horror stories about learning to live with a urine-collection bag taped to her leg, laughing through the memories.

If she could laugh about it, I could, too, right? Maybe someday, at least.

When it happened and I had a room full of detectives asking me questions I couldn't answer, because I still couldn't speak very well even though I didn't have machines breathing for me any longer, and because I didn't want to be forced to think about all the things I'd been through, I wished I could crawl under my bed and not have to come back out for a month. But at least in those instances, the nurses shooed all the detectives out of my room and wouldn't let them come back for a while.

It hadn't happened yet when Ethan was with me, but I knew it was coming. And no matter how well I braced myself against the indignity, I knew there was no way to truly prepare for it.

I'd just have to deal with it when it happened.

And it might very well happen soon, because he was due to arrive any minute if what London told me was true.

I reached for the remote control. They'd looped the cord around my bed rails so I wouldn't lose it and to keep it from getting tangled with all the various and sundry tubes still connected to my body. But once I had the thing in my hand, I couldn't remember which button called the nurse and which turned on the television, so I stared at it for a long time, trying but failing to make my brain work.

"You want to call the nurse?" London finally asked.

I nodded. "I need to pee." The words were so soft I could barely hear them myself, so there was no way the nurse would be able to make out my request on the intercom.

London nodded, though, calm and collected and completely unfazed by my memory lapse. "It's the red button. The big one at the top."

I pressed the button she'd indicated, even though

in my foggy brain, I thought the red button was the one that controlled the television.

Apparently she was right, though, because the TV didn't come on.

The nurse didn't respond over the intercom, either, though. Not for a long time. So long that, whether I'd needed to pee before or not, I really needed to go now, since I was thinking about it.

I pressed the button again, hoping they'd answer soon, because I was sick to death of wetting myself, and even if some of my guests could possibly help me, I didn't think London could. She was in a wheelchair, herself, so how could she get me into one, wheel me into the bathroom, get my clothes off, and help me onto the toilet?

Short answer: she couldn't.

I jammed my finger against the red button so hard that I thought I might break it. It was going to happen. I knew it. My eyes filled with tears of frustration.

London took the remote from me and set it just out of my reach. "I'll go find someone, okay? It'll be all right."

But it wouldn't be all right. That was the problem. *Nothing* was all right, and I didn't think it ever would be again.

I bit the inside of my cheek to stop myself from crying and forced a nod. Then she wheeled herself out into the hall.

A couple of minutes later, my door opened again.

I looked over, hoping to see London and a nurse coming to my rescue, but I completely deflated when Ethan's tall, powerful frame filled the open doorway.

I wanted to see him.

I wanted it more than I should, because I had no business relying on him the way I had been lately.

I just didn't want *him* to see *me*. Not like this.

It was such a contradiction, but I couldn't control the randomness of my thoughts and emotions. They were as much of a mess as the rest of me.

Then I did the worst thing I could possibly have done. The one thing I hadn't allowed myself to do throughout all my time in the hospital.

I burst into tears.

And as soon as I did that, I wet myself again, which only made me cry harder.

Chapter Nine

Ethan

There were a lot of things in life I could handle without batting an eye.

I could handle being a single father and maintaining a good relationship with my kid's mother, despite not being able to make things work out between us within our marriage.

I could handle answering the tough questions my son asked me, even when they made me uncomfortable or when there weren't any good answers to be had.

I could handle being a middle-of-the-road defenseman on one of the worst teams in the entire National Hockey League, knowing it could mean I might never have a shot at playing for the Stanley Cup, because at least it meant I had a good career playing a game I loved and, if I was smart and saved the bulk of my earnings, I should always be able to provide for my family.

I could handle standing up to my own abusive father and the rat bastards who'd done this to Natalie.

But I could not handle seeing her break down in tears in the very same moment I stepped into her room. It felt like she was literally ripping my heart out with each strangled sob and with every tear that dripped onto her hospital gown and turned the delicate baby blue into a deeper shade of sky blue that matched her eyes.

I had never felt more inadequate in my life.

I crossed the room and sat on the edge of her bed, but she shook her head frantically and tried to push me away, so I jumped up again. "What's wrong?" I asked, desperate to brush her tears from her eyes, to sweep the hair back from her forehead, to soothe her in some way. "Tell me so I can help."

But she was crying so hard that she was choking on the sobs and there was no way for her to tell me anything at all.

A weighted sense of uselessness had me collapsing into one of the lavender armchairs in defeat.

Natalie pinched her eyes closed, refusing to look at me.

I felt as if she'd punched me in the gut.

"Do you want me to leave?" I choked out, praying she wouldn't ask me to go. But I would. If she wanted me to go, I would.

But even though she wouldn't look at me, she shook her head *no*.

I took in a relieved breath, still confused, but at least she wasn't going to kick me out.

Her tears kept falling, and she was taking frantic, gulping breaths in an effort to make the sobbing stop, but every time she opened her eyes, she cried harder than before.

London wheeled into the room and stopped next

to me. "What happened?" she demanded accusingly, as if whatever had gone wrong was my fault. "What'd you do?"

For all I knew, she was right and I'd fucked up royally.

"I don't know," I said. "I walked in and she started crying." Talk about a blow to my confidence. And my ego. Yeah, Natalie's crying probably had nothing to do with me, but it sure felt as if it were all about me.

I didn't like that. The thought that I could have done something to upset her made me want to bash my head against the wall.

Natalie caught London's eye and crooked a finger for her to come closer. London wheeled over and bent her head close to Natalie's. I couldn't make out what she was saying—her words were strangled by sobs—but their whispered conversation didn't take long. Within a few seconds, London was nodding and backing away from the bed.

Then she turned around and gave me a sympathetic look. "Why don't you go get a cup of coffee or something?" London suggested. "She'll be fine, and she doesn't want you to leave. Not completely, at least. Just give us a few minutes, all right?"

"I didn't do anything wrong?" I asked, staring at Natalie because I needed the answer to come from her. "You swear it's okay if I come back?"

"Come back," she croaked, still blinking back tears.

"Ten minutes," London said. "At least it shouldn't take any longer than that if I can get a nurse in here to help. Maybe you should knock before you come in, though, just to be sure we're in the clear."

"I'll stop at the nurses' station on my way to the cafeteria and make sure someone's coming," I said. Then, my feet heavy and my heart starting to crack, I backed out of the room and closed the door behind me.

There weren't any nurses at the station as I went past, which was probably why no one had responded yet. Made sense, even if it was frustrating for Natalie.

It wasn't about me. I kept reminding myself of that as I paced through the halls. I was concentrating so hard to remember that whatever had upset Natalie had nothing to do with me that I forgot where I was going and ended up in the maternity ward instead of at the cafeteria.

Several newborns were on display through the windows, with friends and family peeking through the glass and taking pictures of their little bundles of joy. It was such a dichotomy, a stark contrast to the hellish nightmare going on only a short distance away within the same building. New life and unbridled happiness bursting from the seams only a minute's walk away from hellish devastation.

But it wasn't so many days ago that Natalie was a thousand times worse than she was now. I had to remember that. She was recovering at a miraculous rate, at least physically and mentally. Her emotional state was yet to be determined, and I had no doubt it would rebound far more slowly, if ever.

I finally found my way to the cafeteria and fixed a cup of coffee for myself. I grabbed another London, just in case, and picked up a few pastries and a couple of individual-sized cartons of milk. I'd seen the shit they were feeding Natalie, and that wouldn't help her heal any faster. It made no sense to me why the food in the cafeteria for guests was so much more appetizing than what they served patients. Maybe a sugary treat wasn't the best thing for her, but she'd hardly eaten anything since waking up, and I wanted her to eat *something*. And at least the milk would give her some good protein. She'd been losing weight while she'd been in the hospital, and frankly, she didn't have that much to lose.

After paying for my purchases, I loaded them up into a carrier they had handy, then headed through the convoluted hospital corridors and returned to Natalie's room. Since I didn't have any hands free, I kicked at the door with the toe of my shoe to knock. The last thing I wanted to do was walk in while they were changing her or something and embarrass her. And since the door was closed, they might still be doing something that would require privacy.

London opened the door and gave me a cursory once-over. "All better now," she said.

Was it really okay, or was she just trying to appease me? Either way, I raised a brow. "Yeah?"

"It will be if one of those is for me," she said, eyeing the coffees on my tray. "If you're planning to drink coffee in front of me and not share, though, we're going to have issues, you and me. And I'll make sure that also means my husband has issues with you. You don't want to have my surly Russian angry with you. Promise. Maybe you're bigger, but he's meaner."

Surly certainly fit Dima, but I wasn't so sure I'd ever call him *mean*, but I wasn't in the mood to argue with London right now.

She backed out of my way and let me bring my goodies into the room. Natalie cautiously met my eye as I set the carryout tray on the wheeled cart they kept in front of her.

I opened one of the cartons of milk since she seemed to have trouble opening things, and I could have sworn there was a hint of a smile in her expression. It was hard to tell, buried under bruises and swelling and bandages, but her eyes glinted just a bit.

That was the first true sign of life I'd seen in her since the night this had all started—the first indication that she might come out of this on the other side. Not unscathed, and certainly not unchanged, but she was going to pull through.

She was a fighter.

I'd been a fighter, too.

Maybe she wasn't sure what she was fighting for yet. Maybe she'd never know. But I knew what I was fighting for.

I was fighting for her.

Chapter Ten

Natalie

The girls had taped a large calendar onto the wall in my hospital room, close enough to my bed that I could see it whenever I was awake. Every morning, when one of them arrived, she would mark a big red X over that day on the calendar, helping me to see how much longer until I would be discharged.

I had to go to therapy in the mornings, but the girls made sure I had guests every afternoon of my stay, to help keep me calm and sane. I wasn't sure if they'd worked out a rotation to be sure that every day was covered, but whoever was visiting me at any point in time always knew who would be coming next. I was rarely alone other than in the middle of the night when I ought to be sleeping.

Not that I was able to sleep normally. I woke at all sorts of random times, sometimes due to the nurses coming in to take my vitals and other times for no discernible reason at all. I'd lie awake in my bed for hours, flipping channels on the television and hoping to land on something that would distract me from the combination of horrifying memories and the depressing reality I lived in, but it rarely worked.

Most any time of the day or night, I could find reruns of *Criminal Minds* or *Law and Order: Special Victims Unit* playing back to back to back, but I couldn't bear to watch either of those shows for long.

They portrayed events far too similar to the recent happenings in my own life; I didn't need reminders of what I'd been through.

More often, I settled on Food Network, but that only made me hungry for something better than what the hospital cafeteria was feeding me.

Plus, they ran the same infomercials through the late-night and early-morning hours every day, so I'd seen the ads for Cindy Crawford's new makeup line and for the air fryer contraption so many times I could quote them verbatim.

But at least with Food Network shows, I didn't have to think too hard. I could watch without really paying attention, distracting myself from the tedium of so many days cooped up within the same almost-bare walls of the hospital.

I hadn't felt the heat of the sun on my face for what felt like a lifetime, and it was making me crazy—crazier, even, than the drugs that had caused me to hallucinate. And I wasn't entirely sure how much of it had been hallucinations and how much had really happened.

"Did I take my walker and my IV pole and go to the hospital across the street because I liked their nurses better?" I asked Tallie one afternoon.

"No, honey. There isn't a hospital across the street. And no one would let you get out into the hall by yourself right now, anyway, let alone all the way across the street. Do you have any idea what kind of traffic is out there?"

I didn't know anything about the traffic, so I took a look out the window in my room. There was no way I could cross that street with a walker and an IV pole. And there wasn't a hospital over there, anyway. Tallie was right.

Another time, I asked London, "Did someone bring in a bunch of puppies one day?"

"Puppies?" She gave me a side-eye look that said I was crazy.

Maybe I was. But still… "There were puppies climbing all over me and barking and licking me. And one of them peed on my bed and they had to change my sheets again."

"Pretty sure the only one peeing on your bed has been you. And you haven't done that in a while, anyway."

That was true. The more time that passed, the better I was able to control my bodily functions. And with time, I was starting to recognize the difference between reality and what I could only describe as hallucinations.

I never asked anyone about the worst hallucinations—the ones where Hayes and his buddies burst into my hospital room, ripped all the tubes out of my arms, and hauled me away by the hair to start over again where they'd left off.

Although, those might be better described as nightmares than hallucinations.

One afternoon, when I had about a week left before being discharged, a couple of women I didn't know came into my room along with Ethan. A tight knot of worry settled into my chest, until Ethan took a seat next to my bed and reached for my hand.

It felt tiny within his, but I immediately started to breathe more freely. I always felt more relaxed when he was with me. He made me feel safe, somehow, even though I didn't think I'd ever truly be safe again.

"Hi, Natalie," the first woman said, reaching out a hand as if to shake mine, but I could only grasp her hand limply and let her do the shaking. "I'm Joanne Sharp from the district attorney's office. This is Eileen Jacobson. She's a notary who works at the hospital. Mr. Higgins, here, asked us to come to you today so we could help you file a few protective orders against the men who did this to you."

I nodded and struggled to sit up straighter in my bed.

Ethan reached out a strong arm and put it around my waist, almost effortlessly shifting my body into a more comfortable position. Somehow, he always seemed to know what I needed, and he took care of things without even being asked.

Like with bringing these women here to help me out. I hadn't even thought of it, but he'd made all the arrangements already.

They asked me several questions about the various ways Hayes had abused me, how long it had been going on, when Alex and Jason had taken part in it, and the like. I answered, the words coming out of me almost by rote. Speaking about it wasn't anywhere near as difficult as living through it had been. In a way, I felt as if I were floating up above all of this, watching it take place somewhere below me, somewhere in the distance. Was it the drugs still in my system? Or maybe it was because I feared this was just one more of my hallucinations.

Because nothing could truly protect me from Hayes. And certainly not some piece of paper, whether it was issued by the court or not.

But this felt a bit more solid than the hallucinations had, somehow. I'd started to recognize a different feel during the times I was hallucinating, as if everything around me had a strange, shimmering quality.

Nothing was shimmering now. And Ethan's hand was still resting on the bed next to me, his fingers just skimming the edge of my forearm. I could *feel* his presence, strong and soothing, and that never happened in the hallucinations. In them, I was alone, me against the world.

With him here, I never felt alone. I felt protected, almost, even though I knew there was no way for anyone to protect me. Not really.

I finished telling these women my story, and I signed where they indicated. They shook my hand again, and Ethan followed them out into the hall, leaving me alone with my thoughts.

I still didn't know where I'd go once the doctors allowed me to leave, but I was so anxious to get away from the tubes and machines and the sterile smells that I hadn't been able to bring myself to worry about trivialities like that.

I just wanted to be *free*.

Maybe I wasn't behind bars or chained to my bed, but I might as well be, considering my inability to move around on my own. They'd gotten me up and moving some, typically with a walker, but now they were trying to get me to use crutches.

Everything I did hurt. They had my leg in a walking cast, and eventually they wanted me to move on my own without relying on anything for support. But for now, I shuffled from place to place like a geriatric patient following a hip replacement. Actually, I didn't even move as well as most of them. I knew, because there was an eighty-seven-year-old great-grandmother named Maggie down the hall who'd just had a hip replacement, and she was constantly lapping me in the halls, whipping on by so fast the nurses threatened to put speed bumps in her way for her to navigate around.

Moving from my bed to the bathroom and back exhausted me, but they insisted on me making laps up and down the hall a few times a day, just like Maggie.

Taking a shower was an ordeal, what with covering the cast on my leg and the wound on my abdomen with plastic to keep them dry. Plus the soaps and shampoos they had available for me left me feeling itchy. By the time they allowed me to get dressed again, all I wanted to do was collapse in the bed and sleep for a week.

But I was wearing real clothes again now—pj's, really, and a bralette, but still—and every day that went by came with fewer tubes connected to my body and just a hint more freedom. The final thing to go was the IV giving me fluids, and now they had to remind me to drink regularly so I wouldn't end up dehydrated.

I supposed, whether I was ready for it or not, I would have to start thinking about life after the hospital. Not to mention all the hospital bills and how I could pay for them.

The very idea of leaving terrified me, even though I was desperate to get out of this bed, this room, this building, this *life*.

Inside the hospital, I felt safe. Hayes couldn't hurt me in here, other than occasionally when my hallucinations turned to nightmares. But none of that was real.

But out there? How would a piece of paper prevent him from hurting me?

Ethan poked his head back into the room, finally. "Got your papers," he said, moving to take his seat next to me again. He set them down on the rolling cart in front of me. "The judge has to finalize it, still, but that won't take long."

"Thank you," I said, blinking because for some reason I felt the heated prickling of tears trying to force their way through. I didn't want to cry again. I hated crying, and I hated doing it in front of Ethan more than anything.

One of them spilled over, despite my best efforts to keep them at bay.

Instinctively, he reached out a hand and brushed the tear away with the pad of his thumb. It was such a gentle move, such a contradiction, because everything about this man screamed of strength and raw power. How could he possibly treat me so tenderly, with so much care?

He didn't return his hand to my arm, though. I itched for him to touch me in that small way, but I didn't want to ask. I already felt so needy, relying on him and all the WAGs and the nurses to do practically everything for me.

I looked away, because I felt more tears building and I couldn't stand the thought of looking at him while I was falling apart. I didn't want him to see me like this. Broken and battered and bruised was one thing, but this...

This felt different.

Ethan cleared his throat, and I was certain that meant he was about to leave. A tight knot formed in my stomach, fear and nausea and desperation all combining to steal my breath.

But then he surprised me by saying, "Carter and I've been talking about it. And we think you should come and stay with us once you get out of here. I've got a spare room. I can get it set up for you. But we'll still have to figure out what to do when I have to go on the road with the team, because I don't feel good about leaving you on your own. Not while you're still healing. And especially not as long as Lennon's free. Tallie and Dana and some of the other WAGs have said you can stay with them, though, so it won't be too hard to figure something out that'll work for everyone. I've got them sending your bills to me, too," he added, almost as an afterthought.

"You want me to what?" I choked out. I had to have misheard him.

But Ethan looked at me in the same steady way he always did, and there wasn't anything shimmering or out of the ordinary about the way he looked. "Stay with me. And with Carter, when he's in town. So we can take care of you."

Shimmering or not, I had to be hallucinating again. Because this was better than anything I could have dreamed up on my own. "I want to wake up now," I said, and I felt tears stinging my eyes again—tears of frustration this time. This hallucination was going to gut me when I came out of it and realized it wasn't really happening. I couldn't bear to get my hopes up and then have the rug ripped out from under me. Not over something like this.

Ethan gave me a funny look, cocking his head to the side. "You're awake."

"I'm hallucinating. I don't want any more of the drugs that make me hallucinate. Don't let them give me any more." The words came out in a rush, like I was begging, pleading with him to help me. "I can't stand it, Ethan. Please."

"You haven't had any of those drugs in almost a week," he said, his voice strong and steady, just like the rest of him. "They're only giving you pain meds and some stuff to level out your blood pressure because of all the other drugs you've been on. I don't think you'll need to take either of those for much longer, though. Either way, you're not hallucinating. This is real." He reached over and threaded his fingers through mine, holding my hand, grounding me. "Do you feel that?" he asked.

I nodded, tears still burning as they tracked down my cheeks.

"This is real," he said. "*I'm* real. And I'm really asking you to come and live with me. Let me take care of you. Please." His voice cracked on the last word, as if he'd been the one whose vocal cords were sore from having a breathing tube in his throat.

"I'm scared," I choked out.

"Of me?" He looked hurt.

I shook my head. "Not you. I'm really not scared of you. I'm just scared."

"I'd be worried about you if you weren't. You've been through hell. But I want to help make it better. If you'll let me."

How could I ever explain how much he'd already helped me? How he'd already made it better, simply by being here?

"So will you come home with me?" he asked after a charged silence.

I could only nod because that knot in my stomach had shifted and lodged itself deep in my throat.

He didn't say anything for a long time. But then the backs of his fingers stroked my arm, a touch so light I wouldn't have believed it had happened if I hadn't seen it with my own eyes, and he nodded. "Good," he finally said. And if I wasn't mistaken, his voice sounded as strangled and choked as mine.

Chapter Eleven

Ethan

My house didn't have a downstairs bedroom, but there was a game room I'd never used for anything but as a catch-all space for extra storage. A handful of my teammates and their wives helped me get it set up as a bedroom for Natalie in the days before her release from the hospital.

We dragged all the random moving boxes I'd never bothered to unpack out into the garage, and made sure there was nothing on the floors that might trip her or make it difficult for her to get around since she would be on crutches for another month or so.

Hunter Fielding and Eric "Zee" Zellinger were in the midst of assembling a free-standing closet, since there wasn't a built-in closet in this room, while Dima held the directions and grumbled what I could only assume were Russian curse words at them. Razor Chambers and Drew Nash had brought in a bed and were getting it put together while I hung double doors in the open space leading to the living room, with Travis "Prince" Royal, who was currently my defensive partner, and Seth McCormick, an older forward better known as Mac, holding them in place for me.

There was a bathroom down the hall that Natalie could get into easily enough, too, which would be helpful.

But then again, the shower in my upstairs bathroom might be easier for her to get in and out of, aside from the fact that she'd have to climb the stairs. It was a walk-in, as opposed to one that would require her climbing over the walls of the tub.

Honestly, I didn't know which would be better. I'd just have to talk it over with her and see what she preferred. We could figure some of these things out as we went along. However much I wanted everything to be perfect and easy for her, the truth was I didn't have to have all the answers in place before she arrived.

As part of her rehabbing in the hospital, they'd taken her into a mini-apartment that had been set up in the building, helping her to see how she could get around, navigate stairs, and tackle taking care of herself in the kitchen and bathroom. I'd honestly never imagined hospitals did things like that, but it seemed to help Natalie feel more confident about leaving.

While the guys and I took care of the heavy lifting of preparing my house for Natalie's arrival, Tallie organized a few of the WAGs to decorate the makeshift bedroom. They bought bed linens, a rug that shouldn't trip her but would still help with getting traction, curtains, and all sorts of cutesy little doodads to go on the nightstand and some of the other flat surfaces, supposedly to make it feel feminine and home-like for her.

Since none of us wanted to have anything to do with Lennon, we decided not to bother with trying to get Natalie's clothes from him. For all I knew, he'd already gotten rid of them, anyway. Plus, if I ended up within fifty yards of him, I wasn't certain I'd be able to stop myself from ripping out his throat. Better to keep my distance.

Instead, a few of the WAGs who were around the same size as Natalie had pooled their resources and brought over enough comfortable clothes—pj's and other things she could lounge around the house in— to get her through until she was well enough to go shopping. London had brought in a shopping bag with new underthings from some store I'd never heard of, so I could only assume they specialized in women's undergarments.

"No one wants to wear someone's used drawers," she'd pronounced. Reasonable enough if you asked me. I decided not to question her.

All the clothes were already hanging in the closet and folded neatly in the dresser drawers, ready for Natalie's arrival. Now we were down to putting the finishing touches on things.

Dana set out some candles in the bathroom and hung a couple of paintings on the walls, and before long, I didn't even recognize the place. One thing that had been sorely lacking in my life, through the entire time I'd lived in Tulsa, was a feminine touch. Kinsey had always taken care of things like that when we'd been together, but I honestly hadn't bothered with it since we'd split up.

That was one more reason I liked the idea of having Natalie come and live here. For however long it lasted, this arrangement would be as good for me and Carter as it was bound to be for her. We'd have to live like civilized people and not like cavemen.

On the day I was supposed to bring Natalie home with me, Tallie finished off her decorating with a bouquet of flowers she'd picked up on the way over, setting them in a simple glass vase. "Flowers make everything better," she pronounced, rearranging them.

And who was I to argue? If Tallie said flowers would make things better, I was inclined to agree with her. They couldn't exactly make things worse, unless Natalie was deathly allergic to flowers or something.

While I was sure Natalie would appreciate everything we'd done so far, I honestly believed she would be happy with anything at all, as long as it didn't smell like antiseptic and no needles or scalpels were involved. She'd spent so much time in the hospital and had been poked and prodded so much she must feel like a pin cushion. This was bound to be an improvement.

Carter was flying in this morning. He'd been in Michigan with Kinsey for the last couple of weeks, but he had a long weekend off from school that coincided with the T-Birds being at home for a few days, as well as Natalie's release from the hospital. I knew he'd be excited about bringing her home with us. Every time I talked to him, the first thing he wanted to know was how Natalie was doing, even before he asked me about Snoopy.

And while I was on the subject of my son... I made a mental note to remind Carter that he needed to stick to the upstairs bathroom. There would be no crutches slipping in toothpaste on my watch. Boys would be boys, but that didn't mean he had to be a heathen in spaces that would endanger Natalie's safety.

I headed back into the living room to figure out what else I needed to rearrange or tidy up before bringing her into the house. Snoopy barked and followed close behind me. He seemed to be aware that something was changing. With any luck, he'd adapt to the changes as well as the rest of us.

The smell of hot dogs and macaroni and cheese wafted over me, so I followed my nose to the kitchen. London had just brought in a few huge aluminum foil pans full of food that she was putting into the oven.

"Kid food," she said, not bothering to look up at me. "If Carter's anything like my husband, he'll be hungry from the moment he arrives until you put him in bed tonight. This way you can always have something ready for him, since I have a feeling you'll be distracted by getting Natalie settled. There's also some adult food in the fridge. Made a pasta salad, a spinach salad, and there are sandwich fixings. Figured I'd keep it simple for everyone." She wheeled around me with ease, her lap loaded with paper plates and plastic ware, taking those to the dining room table.

"Oh, I almost forgot," she said, glancing over her shoulder at me. But then she angled her head toward the other room, where her husband was still working on assembling furniture with the other guys. "I made brownies. Turtle brownies, with lots of caramel. I put those on the counter. They're for Natalie because she told me they're her favorite. If anyone so much as takes a crumb from that pan before she gets here to eat them, I will personally cut his dick and balls off with a rusty spork, you hear me?" She said that last part with a raised voice.

"You won't cut my dick," Dima shot back, coming into the room with us. Then he grinned and winked at her. "You like it too much."

"You'd better hope you're right if you dare to go near the brownies before Natalie gets here. But maybe you're feeling lucky." She shrugged. "Your loss if you want to test me."

"Viktoriya won't let you," Dima said.

"I think you mean Harper, but I'm not afraid of a two-year-old getting in my way. Viktoriya knows well enough to leave me to my own devices."

"Aren't you the one always protecting Tori and not the other way around, anyway?" Tallie shouted from the other room. "You might just hope she'd protect you."

"My wife's not going to protect anyone's balls but mine," Razor put in, just as Harper Fielding rushed in from the backyard and tugged on Dima's hand.

"Up!" she demanded.

And of course, he immediately picked her up. And she then proceeded to tug on his beard and giggle like the lunatic toddler she was.

"I want a ball!" she demanded, which led to all the guys snort-laughing except Dima, who calmly rolled his eyes and waltzed into the kitchen, sniffing the pan of brownies as if to test his wife.

London brandished a plastic knife in his direction, wheeling toward him with one hand.

I tried not to burst out laughing at those two, but it wasn't easy. They had the most contentious relationship, but somehow it worked for them.

But now it was time for me to go. I had to stop at the airport for Carter before going to the hospital. I shuffled toward the front door, eyeing all of my teammates still hard at work preparing my house for her. A few of the guys had started moving my living room furniture off the rug so they could roll it up and get it out of the way, and I could hear the sounds of others in the bathroom installing a detachable shower head and putting together a shower chair.

A little over two years ago, we'd been a huge band of misfits. Yeah, we were all NHL-caliber hockey players, but we weren't exactly a *team* in the truest sense of the word. But now, everything was starting to come together.

At least off the ice. *On* the ice, we were still struggling to find our identity and the way we fit together.

But if we could keep working together like this, we'd get there.

Chapter Twelve

Natalie

Carter and his dog, Snoopy, stuck to my side the whole afternoon, despite there being numerous other kids around they could have gone off to play with. Every time I shifted positions or tried to stretch out the leg that wasn't in a cast, Carter asked me if he could get me a drink or a snack or if I needed a pillow or if I wanted him to fetch his dad to come and help me get up. One time, he even offered to bring me one of his stuffed animals, "Because my teddy makes me feel better when I'm sick, kind of like Snoopy does."

I'd never spent much time around kids before, but if most of them were anything like Carter, I wouldn't mind doing more of it. He was such a sweetheart. Kind of like his father, only in a much smaller, less intimidating package.

Come to think of it, I was almost positive that Carter's sweet, generous demeanor had an awful lot to do with Ethan's example to him, which was why I was so comfortable around them both. How could any kid be so thoughtful and caring if he didn't have a strong role model in his life to demonstrate that sort of behavior for him? Carter was going to grow up to be a good man, every bit as kind and strong and selfless as Ethan.

By the time midafternoon rolled around, I was beyond exhausted. Every day over the last few weeks, I'd been more active than the day before and stayed up longer, but this was ten times more excitement and activity than I'd been exposed to in the hospital. I tried to keep up with the various conversations going on around me, but my mind kept drifting and my eyes started to close of their own volition, no matter how much I wanted to keep them open.

London startled me awake again by setting a saucer bearing a turtle brownie on my lap and handing me a fork. She placed a glass of milk on the end table next to me. "I wouldn't let my husband have any until you got some, and he's about to drive me crazy. Anyway, it looks like you're done in, so I'm going to make him take his to go. Want me to shove everyone else out the door with him?"

"Oh, I..." I didn't know what to say, because I absolutely wanted everyone to leave so I could rest without feeling bad about ignoring them, but I didn't want to be the one to tell them to go.

She gave me a silent chuckle. "Eat your brownie and leave it to me. I have no problem being the bad guy." Then she backed her wheelchair away from me and let out a whistle that pierced my ears, only stopping when the people closest to her fell silent and turned to look at her.

Snoopy barked excitedly at my side, Carter squinted his eyes and put his hands over his ears, and Harper Fielding blinked at London in shock.

"All right," London said, her voice loud enough to split through the chatter that was still raging. "Time for everyone who doesn't live here to head out. Natalie needs to get her rest, and she can't do that with all of you here."

Within moments, everyone started to get up and gather their things.

Ethan caught my eye from across the room and held my gaze. I wished I could interpret the looks he gave me, but I could never seem to. This one was full of intensity, but why?

Dana Zellinger tossed a bunch of kid things into a large tote bag and handed it to her husband before making her way through the crowd to my side. She handed me my cell phone, which I hadn't realized wasn't in my pocket until that very moment. But then again, I didn't have pockets in the pajama pants I'd worn out of the hospital.

"All of our numbers have been programmed into it for you already," she said. "And we're working on putting together a rotation for when the team's traveling, so you won't be alone. Either one of us will come here to stay with you or we'll bring you to one of our houses."

"And you'd darn well better use it," Tallie added. "Doesn't matter if you got your pants stuck on your cast or if you need company. Call someone."

"I got your number transferred onto my account," Ethan said, alleviating that worry before I could give it voice.

I nodded, blinking hard so I wouldn't start crying. I didn't know what to think of so many people trying to help me out. My own parents had cut me out of their lives a few years ago, when I'd started seeing

Hayes. At this point, I just expected everyone to turn on me. But now that Hayes wasn't in my life anymore, the opposite was happening.

Gradually, they all herded their families out the door—London, Dima, and their little boy were the last to go, with London threatening Dima again because he'd gone back for another bite of brownie—until all that remained were those who would be living in the house and a tornado-like mess.

Ethan looked around for a moment, scanning the chaos they'd left behind before shaking his head and collapsing into a chair. "Cleaning up can wait."

"I can help," I said automatically, determined to do exactly that even though I could barely get myself up off the couch. Actually, that might be an exaggeration. After a couple of attempts at standing, I crumpled back against the cushions in defeat.

I didn't even have the energy to get myself up. How had I lost so much strength in such a short amount of time? It was as if all my muscles had forgotten how to work.

"*You*," Ethan said slowly, eying me from across the room, "can rest. Leave the cleaning to us."

I didn't want to be a burden, though, and I was already feeling like one. "But—"

"But nothing. You're exhausted, and there's no point denying it."

"Maybe you and Snoopy should go take a nap," Carter put in. "He likes naps."

As much as I wanted to argue with Ethan, he was right. I was worn out. No matter how much I'd hated lying in a hospital bed all day, other than the brief times they'd had me in physical therapy or made me walk the halls of the hospital, the truth was I didn't have the energy for much more than that. And being discharged today, then coming to Ethan's house and having most of the team and their families here had combined to drain me—physically, mentally, and emotionally.

I was beyond exhausted, and it had to be obvious.

Ethan pushed up from his chair and crossed over to me, grabbing my crutches on the way. He held out a hand for me, the crutches waiting in the other, and practically lifted me to my feet.

"Thanks," I murmured, taking the crutches from him.

He made sure the path ahead of me was clear and opened the double doors to my room. "You need anything? Some water, or…"

"I don't need anything," I replied. At least not anything he could give me. He'd already done so much more than I ever could have imagined. My arm brushed against his abdomen as I made my way past him. I shivered slightly at the contact.

He waited until I was at my bed and pulling down the covers to climb inside. "I'll make sure Carter lets you rest," he said. Then he closed the door behind him, leaving me alone with nothing but my thoughts.

I wished he hadn't closed the door. I knew he was just trying to give me privacy, but what I needed now was a sense of safety.

I rested my crutches against the wall and sat on the edge of the bed, carefully placing my broken leg under the sheets before arranging the rest of my body.

Until that moment, I hadn't realized how uncomfortable hospital beds were. Yeah, you could raise them and lower them at all sorts of different angles, but the mattresses didn't have much give, and they made me sweat because of the plastic coverings under the sheets. And the sheets weren't terribly soft, a realization driven home by the silky feel of these sheets beneath my fingers.

I tried to get comfortable, to relax enough that I could sleep. Because Ethan was right. I needed to rest if I had any hope of healing and returning to normal. But how could I rest, not knowing what the future held for me?

Yes, Ethan had opened up his home for me and was giving me a place to stay.

For now. But how long would it last? And was I really safe here, or was it an illusion?

I wanted to believe I was safe, and I clung to the hope that Ethan would let me stay at least until I was able to find a job and a way to survive on my own, but neither of us had put any sort of time constraints on our arrangement.

No matter how perfect this seemed on the surface, there was a lot left unsaid. *Too much* left unsaid, to be honest.

On both our parts.

My exhaustion eventually won out, and I fell asleep to the peaceful sounds of a boy and his father playing fetch with his dog in the backyard.

Chapter Thirteen

Ethan

In the few years I'd been playing in Tulsa, the overwhelmingly intense summer heat tended to start dissipating by late September when our preseason games got underway.

Not this year.

September had already come and gone, but we still had temperatures well into the nineties most days, and one day last week, the thermostat had threatened to breach triple digits.

The cooler weather that tended to arrive with fall also usually brought with it some intense thunderstorms, which would mean much-needed rain to soften the parched, cracked earth. Instead, we were still smack-dab in the midst of a months-long drought and heatwave. According to the local meteorologists, there was no end in sight due to a strange weather phenomenon that had occurred in the Gulf of Mexico over the summer.

The high temperatures were holding on far longer than was normal for the area. Air conditioner repair businesses had rarely been in such high demand so late in the year. Most of my teammates and I had only been around for the tail end of the drought, but the locals had been feeling the effects of it since mid-June. My neighbors couldn't recall a drought of this magnitude in recent memory, and they told me heat waves lasting this deep into autumn only occurred every few decades in this part of the country.

I dripped with sweat during each practice, and even more so in games we played at our home arena. The trainers and equipment staff were constantly refilling our water bottles and reminding us to stay hydrated, but cramping and dehydration were still a major concern for almost every guy on our roster.

The BOK Center's air conditioners had to work overtime in order for the ice crews to keep the building cool enough to maintain the ice. It was even more difficult for the guys who had to keep our practice ice frozen since we used it during the heat of the day. That the building maintenance crews managed it was nothing short of a miracle.

Every lawn in my neighborhood looked more brown and brittle than vibrant and green, due to water restrictions that'd been in place throughout the entire state of Oklahoma, as well as almost every part of the southwestern United States, since the early summer months.

The only thing that kept Carter from complaining about the heat when he came down for his weekend visits was taking trips to my teammates' houses—particularly the guys who had swimming pools in their back yards. He and Snoopy swam for hours, wearing themselves out.

Natalie seemed to enjoy those days, even though

she still had to stay out of the water due to her cast. She laughed almost as much as Carter did, especially when Snoopy would leap into the pool and send up a huge splash all over my kid.

Because of that, I encouraged Snoopy to do it some more.

Frankly, I'd do anything to see Natalie smile, to hear the sound of her laughter. There hadn't been much of either in recent weeks.

I kept thinking it would soon be too cool for us to go swimming or to have afternoon barbecues in someone's backyard, but the punishingly dry heat persisted.

A few news crews kept bringing up the Dust Bowl, pondering whether we should expect to experience something of that nature in the coming months or years, which led me to Googling it. After a bit of Internet research, I was reasonably certain they were just fearmongering and that a return of those conditions wasn't something we should expect due to advances in farming techniques, but plenty of locals had already latched onto the idea and were trying to come up with ways to prepare for it. Something told me they were preppers, anyway, so I decided not to give them much credence.

The land around us might be so parched and brittle that it was cracking, but Natalie was not only healing—she was coming to life. Every time I came home from a practice or a game, I picked up on dramatic improvements in her that she seemed to miss.

Her bruises had all healed, now existing only in my memory and in the photographs the hospital workers and police officers had taken as evidence. She was sleeping less and active more, learning to get around without assistance.

But the biggest change was in the way she looked at me when I came home.

In the early days of our new living arrangement, every time I walked in through the front door, there was unmistakable apprehension in her eyes until something in her brain clicked and she realized it was me. Then she visibly relaxed, the anxiety melting away as she sank back against the couch cushions.

No matter how accustomed we got to one another, though, there was always something floating just beneath the surface of all her interactions with me. She was calm in my presence, but a layer of unease and wariness kept her distant.

I understood her wariness all too well—but I didn't know how to explain my understanding without trivializing what either of us had been through. Because of that, I kept it to myself, biding my time for the right moment.

And then one night, a thunderstorm rolled in. The air was filled with the crackling of electricity, and you could *smell* rain, even though nothing had fallen yet.

Carter was with Kinsey, so it was just me, Natalie, and Snoopy at the house when the first crack rumbled overhead. Snoopy whimpered and tried to burrow into Natalie's side on the couch.

"You think we're actually going to get any rain this time?" she asked me.

"If we're lucky." But I kind of doubted it. Lately, we'd been getting storms that were more show than rain. Lots of flashing and banging, but nothing to soak the earth.

Natalie smiled, one of those rare smiles that

actually made it all the way to her eyes. It lit up her whole face, even from across the room. "Wanna go outside and watch? We can sit on the porch."

"You like thunderstorms?"

"Love them. At least the ones we get down here. We didn't get anything like an Oklahoma thunderstorm back home when I was a kid."

She wasn't joking about the storms here. Every spring and fall, I was amazed by the intensity of the fronts that sometimes blew through Tulsa. No Hollywood magic needed here. This was the real deal—thunder, lightning, rain that came down in sheets, high winds and hail, and sometimes even more.

"Yeah, let's go." I grabbed a leash for Snoopy, because I didn't want him to get scared by a crack of thunder and run off, and then I held the door open for Natalie.

She headed out before me and took a seat on the front steps of my porch, leaning her crutches against the railing. I sat next to her, loosely holding Snoopy's leash so he could run off and explore several feet of the yard, his sniffer working overtime because of the crackling energy in the air.

The sun had almost fully set, but the sky was still more purple than black. Dark storm clouds were rolling in from the west, though, ominous and foreboding but somehow promising at the same time.

We desperately needed the rain. I hoped we'd get some.

"Where was home?" I asked, glad to be talking with Natalie about something other than doctors and hospitals and therapy.

Based on her soft sigh of relief, she was glad to be

focused on different subject matter, too. She seemed more relaxed than I could ever recall seeing her before. "Ann Arbor."

"Seriously? Ann Arbor? I grew up in Livonia, so we were practically neighbors. My mom's still up there," I added, almost as an afterthought.

And my father was, too. He was one of the main reasons I never went back if I could help it.

"My family's still there, too. I think."

My brain latched onto the last bit—*I think*. "You don't talk to them?" I asked.

Natalie shook her head, staring off into the distance, where another flash of lightning lit up the night sky. "Not since…" Then she shook her head again.

But I didn't need her to finish that thought. I could fill in the blanks well enough on my own.

"How long did it go on?" I asked.

Natalie blinked a few times, but I could see the flood of tears filling her eyes. She didn't let them spill over, though, somehow holding them inside. I got the sense she had a lot of things locked up tight, keeping them under wraps.

She took a deep breath, refusing to look at me, her gaze never wavering from the electrical show in the heavens. "The first time he hit me, we were seniors in high school. It was right after our prom, actually, so not long before graduation. I had a nasty shiner when I walked across the stage to get my diploma. I tried to cover it up with makeup, but makeup can only do so much."

Another crack of lightning split the sky, followed a few seconds later by a massive, rolling boom that shook the earth, but still no rain fell. Natalie shivered, despite the sweltering heat, but she didn't shift to go back inside.

As long as I could keep her talking, I had no intention of moving a muscle.

"Why did he hit you that time?" I asked. Because if she was anything like me, she would remember every detail. They were all stored in my memory, in a place I kept them tightly under wraps. I could access them when I needed to, but I usually kept them locked away. I'd never forget, but I didn't like to think about any of it too much.

Natalie looked down at her lap for a moment, and I thought I might have pushed too hard, asked for too much. But then she lifted her head and stared out at the rolling clouds again. "Because one of the guys from the basketball team asked me to dance with him, but I was Hayes's date, so I wasn't supposed to dance with anyone but him."

"He hit you because some guy *asked* to dance with you? Not because you danced with him, even?"

"He didn't really need a reason to hit me," Natalie said. "He always gave me one, but he didn't need one. He hit me because he got off on it. That night was also the first night he—"

But then she cut herself off, shaking her head, her lips forming a thin line.

Too soon to go there, apparently. That was all right. At least I had her talking now.

"My father didn't need a reason to hit me, either," I said, not ready to give up on this conversation.

Natalie's head shot around to face me, her brows drawn together, forming a question in her expression.

"My dad beat the shit out of me for years. The first time I remember him hitting me, I was four years old, and I'd come in last place in a race across the pond with a bunch of kids who were older and bigger than me. They'd all been skating for longer than me. He told me that if I ever wanted to play hockey, if I wanted to be someone someday, I had to be faster than all the other kids, and that he'd beat me until I understood."

A fat tear filled one of Natalie's pale-blue eyes, growing to an impossible size before finally spilling over. I couldn't stop myself from reaching up to brush it away with the pad of my thumb. For just a moment, she almost leaned in to my touch, but then she turned away to stare at the light show taking place in the sky, instead.

"Why do you think some men feel the need to hit people?" she asked. Her voice had gone soft and shaky, similar to how it had been after they'd taken the tube out of her throat. "Women and kids, other men? What do they get out of it?"

"I wish I knew. Power?" I suggested. "Maybe they feel like everything's out of their control, and that's how they try to reclaim it?"

"Hayes didn't need to hit me to have control over me," she said, but her voice was almost a whisper.

"He doesn't have control of you anymore."

She blinked a few times, as if trying to stop more tears from falling. "You're wrong," she whispered. "He'll always be there. Always controlling me. He could be in another state or behind bars or even dead, but he'll still be in control."

"Only if you let him," I pointed out.

"He's still out there, though."

"But he's not here." Once the team had suspended him, he'd packed up his shit and left. I didn't know if he'd gone back to Michigan or if he was trying to get a hockey gig in Europe. And frankly, I didn't care, as long as he wasn't here.

"You don't think your dad is still controlling you?" she asked, just as the night lit up like a Christmas tree, with a flash of lightning so bright and intense that it made me jump. The crack of thunder that followed it had Snoopy whimpering and racing back to jump into my arms, burrowing his face in my elbow.

"Not in the ways he wants to be," I said. "He made me who I am today."

Her brow furrowed in confusion, and she shook her head.

"Whether I liked his methods or not, I wouldn't be in the NHL today if he hadn't pushed me the way he did. And it's because of all the shit he put me through that I've made it a point to never, not ever, lift a hand against a woman or a child. My kid's not going to grow up being scared of me. This dog might be scared of thunder, but he's not scared of me. My ex and I couldn't make our marriage work out, but it wasn't because I was abusing her. I wouldn't be half the man I am today if it wasn't for him."

"I don't believe that," Natalie said, and she sounded so sincere it made my chest ache. "You're a good man because of *you*, not because he beat it into you. You're a good man in spite of him."

"But still, he made me want to be better," I insisted. "The way I saw it, I had two choices: I could end up just like him, beating the shit out of my wife and kids, or I could decide to go a different way. 'Two roads diverged in a yellow wood,'" I quoted.

Natalie looked away again, watching the lightshow in the sky. "Did your mother know?" she asked.

"How could she not? He beat her, too. For all I know, he still does. Maybe more than ever since he can't hit me anymore."

"She's still with him?"

I nodded slowly, even though she couldn't see it other than maybe out of the corner of her eye. "I tried to get her to come with me when I got my first NHL contract."

"But she wouldn't come," Natalie said, as if she'd somehow known the answer without me needing to put words to it.

"No, she wouldn't come."

"The same as I wouldn't come with you that first night."

I didn't know how to respond to that. Maybe it didn't need a response.

"Why do we do that?" Natalie asked. "Why don't we try to escape, even when it's that bad? Why do we hope everyone will look away, and why are we thankful when they do?"

There wasn't a good answer for any of those questions. "Fear of the unknown? It's safer to stick with what we know rather than face what we don't know. At least that was what I used to think."

"But you fought back," she said. "You got out."

"You got out, too."

"Only because you saved me."

"Only because you called me for help," I pointed out.

Natalie blinked back some more tears, staring out into the night. It was fully dark now, despite the early hour. The clouds had completely blocked the moonrise. Thunder persisted, sprinkled with flashes of lightning, but there was still no rain.

"Kinsey knew all about how my father beat the snot out of me," I said. "Carter's mom. She knew it well before we got married and had Carter. She witnessed some of it for herself."

"But she was never scared you'd be like him?" Natalie asked.

"Never. You're not scared of me, are you?"

Natalie shook her head.

"Kinsey wasn't, either. She knew me, really knew me. We grew up together. She was the girl across the street. I'd had a crush on her since before I understood what it was to have a crush. I sometimes escaped to her place when the beatings got too bad but before I was big enough to fight back. Her mom would put a steak on my black eyes and other bruises, or sometimes she'd give me a bag of frozen peas to slow the swelling. She cleaned and dressed my cuts. She showed me the kind of love and care I'd never known before. I told her they were hockey injuries. I don't think she ever believed me, but she didn't say anything."

"I told my parents that I fell down the stairs at school the first time I came home with a black eye," Natalie said. "Said my face hit the bannister and that's why I had a shiner."

"Did they believe you?"

She shook her head. "I don't think so. But they never intervened to get me out of that situation. I wanted them to help me. To see through the lies I had to tell them, but no one helped. Not until you."

"People can be really blind to things that are right in front of their eyes."

"But your ex's family saw?"

"They saw, and they knew, but they still didn't step

in to stop him. I think they were afraid of what he'd do to me if they tried to get involved."

Natalie nodded, slow and steady, as if soaking it all in and realizing she wasn't alone. Maybe for the first time since her prom, she didn't *feel* alone.

I wanted that for her. I wanted her to know she had someone she could count on. I needed her to believe she could count on me, that I had some idea of what she'd been through and I'd never allow her to end up in a situation like that again.

"At first," I said, "Kinsey just watched her mother tend my cuts and bruises and shit without saying anything. But then one day, while her mother was dressing a particularly nasty cut on my cheek, Kinsey took my hand and held it in her lap, crying silent tears for me because I refused to let any of my own fall."

Tears much like the ones currently falling down Natalie's cheeks.

"How old were you?" she asked. "When it stopped, I mean."

"I was fifteen the first time I fought back."

"Why then?"

"Because I was finally big enough. He'd pushed me my entire life to be bigger, faster, stronger, better than all the other kids I was playing hockey with. But he never expected me to use it against him." I stretched out my legs just as another crack of thunder had Snoopy diving back onto my lap, shaking in fear. I scratched his ears and tried to soothe him. "One day, I'd taken a bad penalty in a hockey game. On the way home, he got so mad that he pulled off the road and dragged me out of the car, whipping off his belt to beat me with it. But I wrestled the belt out of his hands and used it on him, instead."

"That couldn't have gone over well."

I laughed, a dry, hollow sort of laugh. "That's putting it mildly. He lost his shit. Got back in the car and left me on the side of the road. I was just a kid in nothing but jeans and a sweatshirt on the side of the road in the middle of January in Michigan with no way to get home. I walked a couple of miles to a gas station. Some strangers gave me a few quarters, and I managed to call my coach for a ride. But instead of going back to my place, I moved in with Kinsey's family. And as soon as I got the chance to play in juniors in Canada, I was out of there and never looked back."

"Do you ever wonder?" Natalie asked. "About your mother," she clarified.

"All the time. When I got my first pro contract, I called her and asked her to come live with me and Kinsey."

"But she wouldn't come?" she repeated.

Sometimes, a person needed to hear the same thing over and over and over again before they'd believe it. Before it could sink in. So I said, "No, she wouldn't come. You ever think about your parents?" Maybe understanding that she wasn't alone, that other women in the same position she'd been in, would help Natalie to heal.

"All the time," she said, echoing my earlier response. "But so much has changed now. He cut me off completely. Wouldn't let me have any contact with them, and they refused to have anything to do with him, anyway."

"Maybe you should think about calling them soon."

"Yeah. Maybe." But there wasn't anything in her

demeanor that said she intended to do it, nothing that led me to believe she would go through with it.

It killed me that they'd cut her off when she'd needed them more than anything.

Another streak of lightning lit up the sky, and Snoopy trembled in my arms, but the clouds still refused to release any rain. I scratched him behind his ears, hoping to calm him down.

"Seriously, though, why do you think that is?" Natalie asked. "Why do we stay?"

That was a question she'd have to answer for herself, in the end. I'd already taken one stab at it.

But maybe she just needed to hear it again.

I turned my head until I could meet her eyes. A fresh ache welled up inside me, from wanting to heal her heart but knowing no one could do that but her. "Because we're scared that what we're running to might be even worse than what we're running from," I finally said, not knowing any other answer. "Better the monster we know than the monster we don't know. At least then we know what to expect."

She nodded and stared up at the light show going on in the sky, lost in her own mind.

But I was lost just from staring at her.

Chapter Fourteen

Natalie

I hadn't realized how much I'd come to depend on Ethan since being discharged from the hospital until he had to leave for a road trip with the team.

Physically, I could get along relatively well without him at this point in my recovery; I managed most things necessary to care for myself reasonably well on my own, and the other WAGs were more than capable of assisting me with those things that were still problematic.

But my emotional state was another matter entirely.

Only two days had passed since the team had left, and I felt as though I were falling apart. I thought about Ethan constantly. I missed him more than could be healthy, and it wasn't just because I felt safe when I was with him; I was getting attached.

I had no business getting attached to him.

Ethan had a son and a dog to worry about, not to mention a high-profile career. He'd been incredibly kind and generous to open up his home to me, but I couldn't afford to fall into the trap of thinking this could be anything more than what it was—a good man offering a helping hand to me at a time when I was in desperate need.

If we kept going how we had been so far, at some point, I'd be taking advantage of his sympathy and compassion by continuing to stay. Maybe not yet, but I knew it was coming, and probably sooner than I'd like to think.

Snoopy and I had been staying with London so far during this road trip, but that arrangement was about to come to an end due to a sled hockey tournament her team would be participating in. When she dropped me off at the hospital this afternoon for outpatient therapy, she'd be taking Snoopy over to Ravyn's house, and then she and Erik would be heading out of town for a couple of days. Ravyn would be picking me up later.

London's house didn't have any stairs for me to contend with since she had to get around in a wheelchair, but both of us were constantly checking to make certain Erik, her toddler, wasn't underfoot or in the way of her wheels. He was almost as fascinated by my crutches and the cast on my leg as he was with his mother's wheelchair, which was proving to be an issue.

We both spent an enormous amount of time worrying about crushing his toes under my crutches or getting his fingers caught in the spokes of London's wheels, because that child never stopped moving and sticking his fingers into places fingers didn't belong. He was a quick, sneaky little guy.

One second, he'd have us convinced he was content to play with his blocks and giant Legos on the floor, and the next, he would be climbing the entertainment center and dangling four feet from the ground, seemingly holding on with a single finger and threatening to topple the entire thing over on top of himself.

That child was determined to give us both heart attacks.

It didn't help that Snoopy kept egging the little boy on. Although, his barking tended to alert us that Erik might be doing something he shouldn't be, so I supposed he was helpful in that way, at least.

London was a good influence on me, though, whether I liked to admit it or not. If ever there was someone who deserved to indulge in a bit of self-pity, it was London, but she was constantly reminding me to focus on the things I *could* do for myself and not on those I couldn't.

"Dana told me they're planning to take your cast off this afternoon, before your therapy session," she said conversationally at one point while prying Erik's fingers free from her wheel spokes for what had to be the tenth time in an hour.

"Yeah. They're switching me to a removable walking boot, I think. Something I can take off when I need to, like when I take a bath." And none too soon if you asked me. The itching was killer, and no amount of baby powder seemed to help.

Granted, if my biggest complaint at this point was itching, I supposed I was doing pretty well. Perspective, right?

"That should make it a lot easier to get around."

"And to get clean," I pointed out, laughing.

"That too." She winked. "Maybe you can forget about the crutches soon, then."

"Probably soon. I think I'm going to have to use them to help with balance and weight bearing for a while."

"Still…" She gave me a pointed look, just before reaching around and dragging her son off the entertainment center once again, somehow seeing him out of the corner of her eye. "Progress is progress. Don't knock it."

"Trying not to."

A few hours later, she left me at the hospital for my therapy session and drove off to deliver Snoopy to Ravyn's house before heading out for her tournament. Erik was still giggling and babbling to himself from his car seat in the back.

Before therapy, though, they took me to an exam room to remove the cast. My sigh of relief when they cut the plaster off my leg was louder than I'd anticipated.

The technician chuckled. "Let's get your leg washed and dried, and then I'll get you fitted in your walking boot." She brought in a basin of warm water, as well as towels, washcloths, and soap, then settled in to give my leg a sponge bath.

"I can really shower now?" I asked.

"You can really shower now, as long as you sit in the shower chair. Eventually, you'll be able to stand in the shower if you've got rails. One step at a time, right?"

I nodded. "And I can dip my toes in the pool on a hot day?"

"If you can find a pool that's not all dried up." She winked at me. "Heck, you can get all the way in the pool if you want. Water's gentle on the body. It'd be a good way for you to get some exercise and maybe start to gradually build the strength up in the limb."

Rebuilding the strength seemed an insurmountable task. I couldn't believe how thin my leg had become, just from lack of use. It looked like all the muscle had melted away. Wouldn't surprise me much, considering how much I'd sweated inside the plaster, but still. It was hard to reconcile that this was my leg, the same one that had been so full and fit only weeks ago. Especially when compared to my other leg, which still seemed full and whole and healthy.

Once I was all cleaned up and they'd shown me how to tighten and fasten the hooks and latches on my boot, I spent the next couple of hours going through physical and occupational therapy sessions. Today's focus was on learning how to get around in the boot, which was a lot more difficult than I'd anticipated.

It was definitely nice to be able to walk again, though.

By the time Ravyn picked me up at the end of the day, I was exhausted.

"Look at you!" she said when I met her in the parking lot. "Talk about an improvement."

"You have no idea how good this feels." I was using the crutches for balance but trying to put my weight on my leg, like they'd told me to.

"Mind if we get takeout for dinner?" she asked. "We can pick something up on the way home and eat sitting out by the pool."

"Do I mind?" I almost spluttered. "I am dying to dip my toes in the water." For that matter, I wouldn't mind dipping the rest of me in the water, either. I didn't have a swimsuit right now, but I wasn't sure I'd let that stop me.

"I can imagine."

We stopped at a Chinese place halfway between the rehab center and her house and picked up our food to go. As soon as we got to her place, we both changed clothes—she put on a swimsuit and I dug out a tank top and a pair of shorts.

We took our meal out with us and ate it straight from the Styrofoam containers. Once I was seated, I unlatched my brace and let my legs hang over the edge of the pool, my feet dangling in the water. I let out an indulgent moan almost as soon as the cool water hit me.

"You can get in, you know," she said.

"I know. I will."

Probably.

Maybe.

One thing at a time, though.

I opened my to-go box and dug in, just as Snoopy jumped into the water and splashed us both. We did our best to protect the food from the water, but there was only so much we could do. That dog seemed determined to get us wet. He barked happily and swam all the way across the pool before climbing out on the other side. Then he raced around, his tail wagging like crazy, and repeated the process.

"Better eat fast," Ravyn said.

"No joke."

By the time we finished eating, Snoopy had worn himself out and was floating along on a foam mattress-like thing that he'd confiscated, and the sun was starting to set.

"Wanna get in?" Ravyn asked.

"In this?" I could just imagine the T-shirt clinging to my body. It might even be see-through once it got wet.

"Why not? Who cares? No one's going to see but me and Snoopy."

She had a point.

"I'll help you get out afterward if you have problems."

That sealed the deal for me. I set my to-go box aside and lowered myself into the water, practically groaning at the sensation. The water felt cool and silky on my skin. I hadn't experienced anything so relaxing or indulgent in recent memory.

Ravyn got in, too, after taking care of our trash.

"Don't you worry about the chemicals messing with your hair color?" I asked.

"Nah. It's more work keeping the dreads in good condition than it is keeping the color vibrant."

"What about your tattoos? Don't they fade?" She had more ink on her skin than most of the people I knew combined.

"Sunscreen is your friend when you have tattoos." She swam over to the other side of the pool and grabbed a ball that was floating. As soon as she tossed it, Snoopy leaped off his makeshift bed and swam for it, then brought it back to her. His tail was working overtime.

She tossed the ball for him a few times, focusing on wearing him out, which gave me a bit of a reprieve. Not that she'd been prying or trying to get me to talk about anything, but after spending the day with London and then in therapy, all I could focus on was trying to rest and recover.

Ravyn pushed one of the floating mats in my direction. "Get on that. Put your feet up and relax for a while. You've had a big day. The sun's setting, so you won't burn."

That was more tempting than anything I could've come up with on my own. I shimmied onto it and stretched out, resting my head against the slightly raised pillow and reveling in the sensation of the cool water slipping and sliding over my hips and legs. It was so relaxing that I found my eyes closing, and soon I was dozing off with the water lapping against me.

When I opened my eyes again, it was almost fully dark out. Ravyn had gotten out of the pool and turned on the outdoor lights in the backyard, and she was stretching out on a lawn chair with her sketchpad and pencils. Snoopy had climbed onto my lap and was sleeping, his tail dragging in the water as we drifted.

"Come on," I said, trying to rouse him.

He whimpered in protest.

"I need to get out," I said, laughing, but he didn't budge.

"You're going to have to shove him off you," Ravyn said, not looking up from her sketchpad. "Holler if you need help. He's getting kind of big for that."

It wasn't easy, but I managed to force him off me. He swam over to the stairs and got out, then made another running leap into the water. Apparently, after his nap, he was ready to play some more.

I rolled off into the water and swam over to the stairs. Ravyn had moved my brace and crutches for me already and laid out a couple of towels, so I was able to dry off and suit up again before joining her under the umbrella.

She passed a bottle of water over to me. "You ever think about getting a tattoo?" she asked conversationally, but I got the sense that it was a weighted question.

I took a sip and peeked at her sketchpad.

It was a butterfly, with a ribbon for the body, done in all sorts of shades of teal and purple. She'd thrown in a couple of splashes of pinks and greens for contrast.

I had to swallow hard, because even if I didn't know the specific meaning behind each of the elements, I got the distinct impression that she'd designed this butterfly specifically for me.

"What does it mean?" I asked. I tried to keep my voice level, but it was starting to fade out on me, like it had in the hospital, and I felt choked up.

"The teal in the ribbon is for sexual assault survivors. The purple is for domestic violence survivors. And I thought the butterfly could be you."

I started crying again, which drove me crazy. I was so *over* crying all the time. But there wasn't any way I could have stopped it this time. Ravyn had taken me by surprise so thoroughly that there was no other reaction possible.

She set her sketchpad down on the table, laying her colored pencil on top of it, and passed me a towel since there were no tissues out here. "Good tears or bad tears?" she asked.

"Good tears."

"I thought so. You don't have to give me an answer now. It won't hurt my feelings if you don't want it. And if you wanted something different, that's okay, too. I won't mind or be offended. I just got the inspiration to draw it while you were floating in the pool, and I wanted to make the offer."

I nodded and dried my eyes, and she got up to haul

Snoopy out of the pool so we could go inside.

"Where would you put it?" I asked, but only after I trusted my voice enough to chance speaking.

"Anywhere you want it. You can have it somewhere it's hidden and just for you or somewhere you can show it off. There are lots of possibilities we could explore. I've done some pieces for women who've had mastectomies, and they cover the scars. We could do something to cover one of your scars if you wanted. Not right away—you've got to let the scar heal for about a year first, at least. Anyway, no need to make up your mind now. Let's dry off and clean up so we can get inside and watch the game."

I gathered up the towels and trash from our meal, tidying our mess while Ravyn did her best to dry the dog. But I couldn't stop thinking about the design.

Before we went into the house, I took out the cell phone Ethan had given me, and I snapped a picture and sent it to him in a text message, asking for his opinion. He probably wouldn't answer until late tonight, because they weren't allowed to have their phones on so close to game time.

But he surprised me by responding almost immediately.

It's gorgeous. But so are you.

I tossed my phone onto the pile of stuff we needed to carry back inside, but now I had the faint hint of a smile trying to break free, and I didn't think I'd be able to stop it.

And to be honest, I didn't want to stop it.

Chapter Fifteen

Ethan

It'd been ages since I'd felt this sort of itch to get home from a road trip.

Back when Kinsey and I had been together, maybe. Or occasionally if I was missing Carter and knew he'd be flying down for a weekend visit, but these days we used Facetime almost every day, so the ache didn't get to be too bad.

But being away from Natalie for the past five days had been torture.

I told myself it was just because I was worried about her—how she would handle staying with the other WAGs and moving from house to house while I was gone, how she was getting along in therapy, whether Hayes would attempt something despite the protective order she had against him—but in truth, it was more than that.

I still wasn't ready to give what I was feeling a name, especially because Natalie wasn't ready to jump into another relationship. Hell, she might never be ready for that, and I refused to be the asshole who pushed her into anything she didn't want, no matter how I felt about her. I cared too much to do something like that. She deserved better. And if I pushed her into something she wasn't emotionally prepared for—or possibly even worse, something she didn't want—it wouldn't be good for either of us in the end.

There was no getting around the fact that I'd been insanely distracted on this road trip, though, and it was making itself known through my performance on the ice.

Doug Spurrier, our head coach and a guy better known around the league as Spurs, held me back after the morning skate before our game against the Portland Storm—the final game of this trip. He watched the rest of the guys heading off the ice, waiting until we were alone.

"You're playing tonight," he said, taking his time and carefully measuring his words, "but you're not going to get too many more chances. At least not in the short term. I know you've got a lot on your mind. I understand you're worried about Natalie, and with good reason. But you've still got a job to do. I can't allow you to jeopardize games for the entire team just because you're distracted. Everyone has shit going on at home, but we all have to do our parts. We've got to start off this season on the right foot."

"I know. I'm sorry." I dragged a hand down my face, three days' worth of stubble scratching my palm. "I'll get it under control."

"Foul up tonight, and Ike will be taking your place against Vancouver."

Ike was what the guys all called Isaac Johnson, who was our seventh defenseman these days. He hadn't gotten into a game yet in the regular season, so he was due to get some ice time, anyway. But I didn't want it to be at my expense.

"That won't be necessary," I insisted. And I intended to make sure of it.

"Get your shit together, Bear."

I nodded, and he sent me on my way.

Bear was what most of the guys called me these days. It started out being *Huggy Bear*, a play on my last name and my size, I supposed, not to mention my tendency to be a bit standoffish and quiet. In general, I kept myself to myself and minded my own shit. While they rarely used the *Huggy* part of it anymore, *Bear* remained.

I showered and changed, then ordered room service instead of going out with any of the other guys.

Prince and a few of the younger guys were having lunch in the hotel restaurant and had invited me to join them. Wasn't interested, though.

Zee, Razor, Hunter, and Andrew Jensen had asked me to tag along with them—they all used to play here in Portland, and they were meeting up with a bunch of their former teammates for lunch at some Italian place called Amani's to catch up on old times—but I wasn't in the mood to be around anyone unless that someone happened to be Natalie. And since she was in Tulsa and I was in Portland, I figured I was better off keeping myself company instead of dragging anyone else down with my moodiness.

While I was eating, I took out my phone and checked the messages I'd missed.

Kinsey had texted me a few pictures of Carter hanging out with some friends at a water park. He was acting like a complete goofball, totally hamming it up for the camera, which made me laugh. My kid was a character.

There was a quick text message from Natalie, just three simple words: *I'm doing it*. No doubt that meant she was letting Ravyn give her that tattoo. I was curious to know where she was putting it, but she might not want to tell me. I sent a thumbs-up emoji and a couple of hearts as a response. She could show me if she wanted, or not. Totally up to her.

Then I checked my email, but almost immediately wished I hadn't.

Someone from the district attorney's office had sent me a notice that Lennon's two friends had both managed to come up with the required bail money and had therefore been released on their own recognizance. So now all three of those bastards were out and about, but I was halfway across the country and there wasn't anything I could do if they decided to give Natalie a hard time.

Yeah, she had protective orders against them, but honestly, those orders were nothing but scraps of paper. If any one of those sons of bitches wanted to do something to her—to make her pay for the fact that they'd gotten caught—there wasn't anything a protective order could do to stop them.

I shot off a group text message to all the WAGs who were helping to look after Natalie while we were on the road. I'd barely hit *Send* when the knock sounded at my door, signaling the arrival of my lunch.

Tossing my phone onto the bed, I crossed over to answer the door.

But my food wasn't all that was waiting for me. Mac, who happened to be the other divorced father on the team, was leaning against the wall, as if he'd been waiting for me. He had a to-go bag in his hands from one of the restaurants that I'd seen down the block from the hotel. "Mind if I join you?" Mac asked.

I shrugged and took my tray inside, letting him follow me. After setting my tray on the table by the window, I took a seat and dug in.

Mac stretched out his long legs on the couch and ate straight out of his bag, without even bothering to take all his food out. "Do you ever think you fucked up getting married and having kids so young?"

"I was young, but I wasn't *too* young," I said, pouring the balsamic vinaigrette over my spinach salad. "I knew what I was doing. What I wanted. Twenty-four when Kinsey and I got married. We had Carter a year later."

"Shanna and I were eighteen. Stupid fucking teenagers," he said. "Got married straight out of high school—not even a month after graduation. Neither of us had ever dated anyone else, even."

"But you loved her, though, didn't you?"

"Yeah, but it was never going to last. We should've seen it. Everyone else did, and they were all too happy to tell us how stupid we were, especially once we'd divorced. We didn't have a fucking clue. Just got married so fast because she was pregnant and we figured that was what you do, right? I signed my first contract, and we kept having babies. A few years later, we had three kids to raise but we barely knew each other anymore. I was being shuttled around in the minors and she was changing diapers and trying to keep toddlers from eating dog shit in the backyard. That was bad enough, but now they're fucking teenagers. All three of them. How the hell did I end up with three teenagers? I'm not old enough for this shit."

I smothered my laugh because Carter would be a teenager at some point, too, and there was no telling what that would entail. My boy was a good kid, but hormones could fuck with anyone. Didn't want to end up with Mac having earned the right to say *told ya so*. Maybe he wouldn't, but... Nah, he would. He totally would. And he'd probably take a swipe at me now for laughing.

For the next couple of hours, I listened to Mac whine and complain about all the crap he and his ex were going through in trying to raise three teenagers, especially when they didn't see eye to eye on all of it, and I did my best to absorb as much as I could for when Carter was that age so I'd have a leg up on whatever issues Kinsey and I might run into.

But then, finally, blessedly, Mac had to head back to his room so he could dress for tonight's game.

As soon as he was gone, I checked my cell phone.

There were several responses from the WAGs, letting me know they'd gotten my message and would be doubly aware of everything going on around Natalie. Tallie said she'd made a call to the local police station to get a list of dos and don'ts to pass around to all of them, which wasn't much, but I supposed it was something.

But then I got to a message from Natalie. *I got it*, it read, which had to mean she'd gotten the tattoo, but there was no photo attached and no mention of tattoo placement, or even if she liked it.

I tapped out a quick response: *Can I see?*

Almost immediately, she came back with: *Not now.*

I'll show U when U come home.

So now I had to wonder—did she want to wait until I was home because she didn't want pictures floating around? Was it somewhere she didn't want photographic evidence of? Or maybe she hated it. In all honesty, it was probably just because she still had to have it covered in plastic wrap, so it wouldn't photograph well yet.

But my brain wouldn't settle on the easy, most likely reason. My mind was going a mile a minute.

I couldn't wait to get home.

......

For the better part of last season, Prince and I had been defensive partners. So far this season, the coaches seemed content to keep the pair of us together, which was fine by me. Pretty sure Prince was okay with the arrangement, too. I had plenty of size and could use it to our advantage. He was a bit on the smaller side (at least in comparison to me) but significantly better at moving the puck, not to mention scoring, himself.

As a partnership, we were relatively well balanced. I took care of banging bodies to keep them out of our goaltender's way, and he took care of corralling the puck and getting it into the forwards' hands.

We didn't even need to talk to each other very much, which worked out fine for both of us. Actually, Prince didn't talk much at all, no matter who was around or what was going on, and I'd much rather someone else do the talking most of the time.

On the ice, we tended to let our game play speak for us. It worked out well for us and the team as a whole.

Usually.

Tonight was proving to be an exception to the rule. Which, if we were honest with ourselves, we should have expected. The Storm had been one of the better teams in the league for half a decade or more. They were always in the playoffs, perennially one of the bigger threats in the Western Conference.

We weren't quite bottom of the barrel now that we'd been in the league for a few seasons, but we might as well be. I doubted we'd even get to sniff at the playoffs for at least several more seasons.

At the moment, Prince and I were getting a front-row seat to witness *why* our opponents for the night were so damn good. Better than front row, actually, since we were on the ice and trying to stop them from scoring for the third time this period.

They'd thrown out their top line of Riley Jezek, Jamie Babcock, and Nate Golston. Prince and I were both already far past the point of being winded, but we were stuck in our defensive zone and couldn't get the puck out so we could get off the ice for a change.

Jezek and Golston might as well be fucking twins, because they could read one another like they'd shared a damn womb. Babcock seemed to have eyes in the back of his head when he was playing with those two; he always knew where the puck would be without needing to turn his head to look for it. The damn thing just landed right on his tape the second he put his stick on the ice.

"Clear it out of here," Hunter shouted at me when I skated past him to dig the puck free from the corner.

What the fuck did he think we were trying to do?

I didn't waste the breath necessary to roll my eyes at him; I needed all the oxygen I could get to deal with the Storm's top forwards.

But no sooner did I get the blade of my stick on it than Golston was there. He was like a pesky gnat that just wouldn't go away. I fucking hated playing against guys like him—small but strong as a fucking mule, and more determined than the runt of a litter trying to get to a free teat at feeding time. Golston was one of the shorter guys in the league, and I was almost the tallest. If I hit him the way I hit most anyone else, it'd be a fucking elbow to the head or something, and I'd be suspended faster than I could blink. He played with the attitude of a guy twice his size, though, like a chihuahua going up against a Rottweiler.

I tried to kick the puck free with the toe of my skate, hoping to send it in Zee's direction, but Golston blocked it with the blade of his stick.

Mac skated over to help out, but adding his stick to the mix only created a bigger blockade, trapping the puck in place. Finally, Mac managed to tie up Golston's stick with his own, and I squeaked the puck out of the pile, but I got too much juice on it. The fucker squirted past Zee and all the way down to the other end. Storm defenseman Keith Burns got to it first, and the refs blew the whistle as soon as he got his stick on it.

Icing. Lovely.

They sent out fresh legs, but my teammates and I were all stuck out there, winded and exhausted and needing to get off for a line change.

We lined up for the face-off, all huffing for air and sweating like crazy.

The linesman dropped the puck.

Zee put up a good fight for us, but Storm center Blake Kozlow tied up Zee's stick with his own and kicked the puck over to one of his teammates with his skate blade. We all scrambled to get into position, Prince chasing Kozlow into the corner and me taking up position in front of Hunter, but—winded and out of gas—we were no match for their fresh legs.

Their forwards got off a couple of crisp passes, dragging all of us out of position. Their left wing fired a wrister on Hunter, which he stopped but only by flailing in an unorthodox move that left the net wide open. Their center somehow freed the puck from the pile of bodies that included both Hunter and Prince. He surveyed his options and then Leif Sorenson, one of their defensemen, lifted his stick for a slapper.

Hunter would never get back into the net in time. I had no choice but to drop to the ice and pray the puck hit me.

It did. Right on my cup. I felt the cup crack from the force just before I felt intense pain starting in my balls and radiating all the way down to my toes.

Thank fuck for that plastic invention. I could only imagine how a ninety-plus-mile-an-hour slapshot to the balls would feel without protection.

In too much pain and shock to move, I collapsed, but the puck was under me.

Hunter flailed around, shoving me off the puck so he could cover it himself, and we finally got a whistle.

The officials moved in to separate all the bodies in front of our net, and Zee and Prince helped me get to my feet. I knew there had to be tears in my eyes, but fuck. I'd been kneed in the balls once by a girl in middle school, but that had been nothing compared to this.

They each threw one of my arms across their shoulders and helped me to the bench, and one of the other guys opened the door so I wouldn't have to climb over the boards.

Jesse Coakley, our head equipment manager, made his way down the bench and leaned over. "Good thing for cups, eh?"

I couldn't speak. No chance. I couldn't even nod my head.

"At least you've already got a kid," Mac joked as he jumped onto the ice. "Might have permanently damaged your swimmers."

As the trainers took me off the bench and helped me back to the room to be examined and evaluated, I didn't even have it in me to tell him to go fuck himself.

Chapter Sixteen

Natalie

"Seriously, how can you stand having ice on that?" I asked, half-amused, half-shocked. "I'm trying to imagine putting ice on some of my more private areas, and...no. Just no. I couldn't do it."

Ethan laughed into the phone, which made my belly flutter in a way I didn't want to examine just yet. "It's not easy at first. But I promise, it's better having it numb."

"Yeah, but the time between when you first put the ice in place and when it goes numb... I don't know."

It was the middle of the night, following the Thunderbirds' loss to the Storm. Ethan had texted me once he was back in his hotel to see if I was still awake, and I'd called as soon as I saw the phone light up with his name. I was trying to keep my voice down so I wouldn't wake Viktoriya if she was sleeping, but there wasn't a chance I'd pass up the opportunity to talk to Ethan right now.

"Playing with ice can be sexy," he said.

I clammed up, suddenly hot and flushed all over, so hot that some ice on my skin wouldn't be uncalled for. How could I already be feeling this way toward any man? It seemed too soon, especially since I hadn't been sure I'd ever want another man's touch again. But now I was thinking about Ethan, and his big, strong hands and how safe and protected he made me feel, and suddenly, there was something more.

"I've had worse injuries," Ethan said, changing the subject before my thoughts could completely run away with me, before I could say something I might regret. "And so have you."

"True, but still."

"You could ki—" he started to say, but then he cut himself off suddenly.

"I could what?"

"Nothing. Forget I said anything."

"That's not going to happen, and you know it. I could what?" Something that started with a k-sound. Kick him in the balls? Doubtful since he was already hurting so much, anyway. And regardless, I would never do something like that to him. But what?

"I was about to say something really crass and totally inappropriate, and I realized my mistake before it was too late, all right?"

Crass and inappropriate? That didn't seem like the Ethan I knew at all, but...

"I could kiss your boo-boo and make it better?" I suggested, unsure where the boldness had come from. Because if he had been here, in front of me, there wasn't a chance I would have said anything of the sort. Somehow, with him being halfway across the country, I had done it, though.

And I was almost certain that was exactly what

he'd been thinking, what he'd almost said.

And I was fairly sure that he wanted it as much as I did.

Almost. Maybe I only hoped he did. Maybe I was reading something in him that I *wanted* to be there even if it wasn't actually there.

He might not want me. He might just be a kind man, someone who'd help anyone in a similar situation, and his kindness didn't have anything to do with *me*, per se. Actually, that might be the truth. Ravyn had told me how Ethan and Carter had ended up with Snoopy. They'd found the puppy tied up in a garbage bag, left on the side of the road. I might just be the latest stray he'd taken in.

But now I'd said it, and it was out there, dangling between us like forbidden fruit in the garden of Eden. Now, everything was going to change.

It had to, whether for good or bad.

"Natalie," he said on a sigh, and he sounded strangled and frustrated, and there was a hint of something else in his tone, but I couldn't put my finger on what that something might be.

"Sorry," I forced out. "Forget I said anything." But I knew better than to think either of us could do anything of the sort. I couldn't unsay the words. Besides, I wasn't sure I wanted to, even if I could.

"You know I don't expect—"

"I know," I cut in. But why was he trying so hard to convince me his intentions were strictly honorable? Maybe I didn't appeal to him, especially after what Hayes and his buddies had done to me. A sharp, aching pain stabbed me in the gut, and I had to blink back tears. "I shouldn't have said that. Please, try to forget I did."

"I can't do that," he said.

I pressed my eyes closed, thankful he wasn't here to see me cry. "I'm so sorry," I said.

"Don't be sorry. I mean I can't forget it because I want it so much. I want *you*, but I feel like an asshole for wanting you when you're still so hurt, so raw. When you're still dealing with so much."

"You want to be with me?" I asked, my tongue so thick that the words were strangled.

"More than I should. More than I ever imagined possible. But most of all, I want you to be healthy. To be happy. To be safe."

"I feel safe with you," I said. "I miss you." There was so much more I wanted to tell him, so much I needed for him to know. But if I tried to speak more now, it would all come out as a massive sob.

But I got the sense that there were just as many things he'd left unsaid as I had, just as many things stealing his ability to speak.

"I miss you, too," he said after a painful silence passed between us. "I need you to know that I'm never going to push you, though. I'm never going to put what I want ahead of what you need."

"What if it's what you need, too?"

"It's got to come from you, Nat. It's all got to start with you."

So, the ball was in my court? That was how it seemed.

Now the question was: what did I intend to do with it?

Chapter Seventeen

Ethan

Carter's flight to Tulsa was due to land about forty-five minutes after the team's flight landed, so I took my bags to my car and then headed back inside to wait for him. I'd barely made it through security and reached his gate by the time he was skipping down the bridge, holding hands with a flight attendant with his Tow Mater backpack dangling from his free arm. The flight attendant was carrying his suitcase—which was, of course, a Lightning McQueen suitcase, because Mater and McQueen were best buddies, just like Carter and Snoopy.

"Dad!" he shouted. He ran straight into my arms, ignoring the flight attendant's admonishment that she needed to check my paperwork first to verify that I was the adult legally allowed to pick him up.

I passed the papers over to her with one hand, the other wrapped tightly around my kid because he had a death grip on my neck and obviously had no intention of letting go. She chuckled and took the paperwork from me, giving it a quick once-over.

"Did you have a good flight?" I asked him.

The flight attendant winked at me and handed all the paperwork back with a knowing smile.

"The man next to me let me watch *Monsters, Inc.* on his iPad," Carter said.

I took his suitcase from the flight attendant, re-situated Carter's backpack over both of his shoulders so it wouldn't fall off him, and grabbed hold of his hand to lead him out of the airport. "That was nice of him," I said, but I thought to myself that my son's seatmate was probably just trying to have a little peace and quiet on the flight. Carter could talk anyone's ear off if he was in the right mood for it. "Did you say thank you?"

Just like that, my son stopped cold. "Oh no. I forgot." Then he turned around, scanning the sea of faces. He climbed up on an empty chair for a better angle. "I don't see him!"

"He probably went to baggage claim," I said, holding out my hand again.

But Carter refused to be swayed. "We gotta go find him."

I laughed to myself, but I said, "All right. Let's go see if we can find him. We have to go past baggage claim to get to the car, anyway." This time, when I reached for Carter's hand, he took it.

We gathered up his things again and started the long walk to get out of the building. He made up a game as we went, designating where it was safe for me to step and where I might trigger an attack of the monsters from his movie, despite the fact that we were wide awake and the scary monsters were supposed to come out while you were sleeping.

"You need to use the bathroom?" I asked when we were almost at baggage claim, since I spotted a sign out of the corner of my eye. "Might be a while before we can get to another one."

"I went *pee* on the *plane*," he said, sounding like it was an absolute coup, the best thing he'd ever experienced.

"Got it," I said, chuckling to myself. "Did you remember to wash your hands?"

"Duh," he said, but he sounded guilty.

I made a mental note to make him use a wet wipe as soon as we got out to the car. And I'd be using one for myself, too.

We finally reached the baggage claim area. I checked the overhead signs to find where Carter's flight would be receiving their bags, and then we headed for that carousel.

He craned his neck to see around the crowd of bodies, trying to catch sight of his seatmate. Before I could stop him, he'd climbed onto a chair again so he would have a better vantage point. "There he is," he said, jumping down and taking off before I could stop him.

With his size, he was able to wind through the sea of bodies with ease, but it was a bit harder for me to make my way through the crowd. I kept my eyes fully trained on my kid, though, and by the time I caught up to him, he was already tugging on a man's hand.

But when the man turned to him, annoyance creasing his brows, my heart stopped.

Because it was my father.

He was older, grayer, more wrinkled, but he looked every bit as mean. I'd seen that look he was giving my kid more times than I could count.

I shoved the last couple of bodies out of my way and lifted Carter into my arms. "We've got to go," I ground out.

"I just wanna say thank you!" Carter complained.

"Not now," I bit off.

"Not gonna say hello to your old man?"

"Dad!" Carter squirmed in my arms, trying to get free, but I only held on tighter. Almost so tight I would hurt him. I had to force myself to loosen my grip, because the only person I wanted to hurt in this situation was my father.

As calm as I could force myself to be, I said, "I don't have anything to say to you. You'd better stay away from me. And you stay the fuck away from my kid, too. You got that? What the hell are you even doing here, anyway?"

"Got a call from a lawyer," he said. "Wanted me to come down and testify about how you like to tell stories. How a couple of disciplinary spankings because you mouthed off at me and your mother got blown up into me supposedly beating you, so you're probably telling these same stories now about some chick. Your teammate's girlfriend, right? You sleeping with her? That what this is about? Wanted to screw some other man's girl, so you felt the need to make him out to be the bad guy? We all know you've got a history of telling flat-out lies just so you can get attention."

I don't know how I mustered the necessary restraint, but I carried my squirming son and his suitcase out into the muggy Tulsa air without putting my fist through that bastard's face.

"Dad?" Carter said once we were outside. He sounded scared.

Fuck, but that son of a bitch had made me scare my kid.

I set Carter down on his feet and dropped to my knees so I'd be closer to his level. "I'm sorry about that, buddy."

"Is that man your father? Is he my grandfather?"

"He is," I said slowly, because I was *never* going to lie to my son. Not if I could avoid it.

"Why did he say that? Why did he say you lied?"

I looked him in the eye, fighting a war in my own mind. How much should I tell him? He was just a kid. I wanted him to *stay* a kid, and not have to experience so many of the shittier aspects of the world we lived in. But Carter had seen what Hayes had done to Natalie, so he'd already been exposed to so many things I'd rather he never saw. I owed him the truth.

"You remember how Miss Natalie's boyfriend hurt her?" I started.

He nodded.

"Well, my father used to hurt me the same way."

"But he was your dad!" Carter said, outraged and shocked.

"I know it. But not all dads are good. Sometimes, people do really awful things to other people, to the same ones they should love the most."

He sniffled, but he reached both arms around my neck and gave me an enormous bear hug. "I'm glad you're my daddy," he said, his voice muffled in my neck.

I picked him up, got to my feet, and carried his Lightning McQueen suitcase since the handle wasn't anywhere near long enough for me to bother with the rollers. "I'm glad I'm your daddy, too," I said.

But now I had one more thing to worry about.

Because Hayes, the rat bastard, was trying to discredit
me.

Chapter Eighteen

Natalie

Carter rushed through the door and wrapped me up in a bear hug almost as soon as Ravyn let them in. His arms tightened around me in a death grip. I'd expected him to go for Snoopy first, so I wasn't sure what to make of his behavior. For that matter, I hadn't expected him to hug me, at all.

"Hey," I said, patting him on the back and looking up at Ethan for an explanation. "I missed you, too."

But Ethan seemed angry and closed off, his dark brow creased and his lips set in a thin line, so I didn't think I'd be getting answers from him any time soon. Maybe I could coax it out of him once we were back at his place and Carter was in bed. I certainly intended to try, although whatever was upsetting him might not be any of my business. Maybe it was something to do with Carter or his mother, family matters.

I wasn't part of the family, whether I lived with them or not.

Something told me it was more likely a response to our phone conversation, though. I'd gone and screwed up a good thing. No matter how much he tried to convince me everything was fine, I'd known that I'd made a mess of things by awkwardly flirting with him. I should've thought before I spoke, but now it was too late, and I wasn't sure if I could repair the damage I'd done in our relationship.

Snoopy barked a few times and nosed his way between us to lick his boy, and in no time, Carter was giggling and rolling around on the floor while Snoopy jumped all over him. Their exuberance was endearing and infectious.

I wished I could let go and enjoy life the way those two did.

I itched to feel Ethan's arms around me, a cocoon of warmth and refuge, but he was taciturn and standoffish, separate from the happy reunion. And it was my fault. Everything was going to be awkward between us, and I wasn't sure there was a way for me to repair the damage I'd caused.

Things had to change between us after that phone conversation, but I hadn't expected the transformation in his demeanor to be so sudden or so cold. To keep from crying over the unexpected shift in our relationship, I focused on Carter and Snoopy.

Ethan gestured to Drew and Ravyn to follow him into the kitchen. I was tempted to go with them even though I hadn't been invited, my curiosity almost overwhelming in its intensity, but I stayed put.

Whatever it was, if he wanted me to know, he'd tell me. I had to believe that.

He'd been up-front to this point, so there was no reason for me to expect anything else.

They returned a couple of minutes later, and Ravyn caught my eye and gave me a gentle smile, as though to soothe my nerves. It did nothing of the sort.

But then Ethan finally met my eyes, and his demeanor was wholly changed, to the point that I had to question whether I'd misread him entirely. "You ready? I promised Carter we'd order pizza tonight. Hope that's all right."

I nodded in surprise, my tongue too thick to form words.

"Can you get all of Snoopy's things while I help Miss Natalie?" Ethan said to his son. He didn't wait for an answer, picking up my duffel bag and holding out a hand to assist me to my feet.

His quiet strength somehow warmed my entire body, despite our only contact being through our hands. The power in his hand ought to terrify me, but instead I was drawn to it. To *him*. I felt an indescribable urge to feel his hands on my flesh.

How was it possible to desire any man's touch after all the things Hayes had put me through? How could I want from Ethan what terrified me when coming from Hayes? I didn't understand myself, my feelings and longings.

I stood and picked up my crutches, my nerves still on edge. I wished I could read Ethan better. I wished I could guess what was going on inside his head, but he kept a tight rein on his thoughts, leaving me guessing.

Carter kept up a constant stream of chatter the whole car ride back to Ethan's house, which forced me out of my brooding and into a slightly better frame of mind. Once Ethan had parked in the garage, he and Carter unloaded everything from the trunk while I cautiously made my way inside the house, careful not to accidentally place one of my crutches on Snoopy's paws—no easy task since he was racing happy circles around everyone.

The guys followed us inside a moment later.

Ethan carried my duffel bag into my room, dropping it on the foot of the bed before taking all of his and Carter's things upstairs. Carter immediately headed into the dining room and put fresh food and water into Snoopy's bowls. Something told me this was their usual routine, each of them doing their assigned tasks without need for discussion.

When Ethan returned, he said, "Why don't you and Snoopy go outside for a bit, buddy? Go run off some energy."

"Should I turn on the sprinklers?" Carter asked.

"We're still on water restrictions," Ethan replied. "But it's early enough in the day we can get away with it for a bit, I think. And the yard could use some water. If you're going to do that, put on some swim trunks first."

Carter raced up the stairs with his dog hot on his heels.

"Thought we could use some quiet to talk," Ethan said softly. "There's something I need to tell you."

I nodded, my stomach in knots. What did he need privacy to say? What couldn't be said in front of his son? But Ethan took a cushion from the couch and set it on the coffee table in front of me before gently lifting my broken leg to rest upon it.

Then, without another word, he headed into the kitchen. I heard the faucet running, the distinct sounds of him taking something down from the cabinets, of loading the dishwasher and moving items from the freezer to the fridge. Busy work. Tasks to soothe his mind and clear his thoughts?

Carter and Snoopy thundered back down the stairs and raced past me into the backyard. At first, he forgot to close the sliding glass door behind him, but he doubled back after a moment and slipped it closed, giving me a sheepish expression.

After what felt like an eternity, Ethan returned to the living room with two bottles of water. He passed one over to me before taking a seat across the room from me.

I'd hoped he would sit beside me. I craved his nearness more than I could stand.

To distract myself from the uncomfortable line of my thoughts, I opened the bottle and took a sip.

"My father's in Tulsa," Ethan said.

I nearly spit out the water in shock. "What? Why?"

"He was on Carter's flight. Sat next to him the whole way down, even. He let Carter watch a movie on his iPad."

I could only blink, my confusion stealing my tongue.

"Hayes's lawyers brought him in to help them put together a defense," Ethan said, his voice devoid of all emotion.

My heart dropped into my stomach.

"He's going to tell them I made shit up about all of his abuse. That I'm obviously just making shit up now about Hayes because I wanted to steal you from him or something else equally ridiculous."

"But the video," I spluttered.

"Hayes isn't on any of the footage. Only his buddies are. So we might be able to still have a case against them."

"But not Hayes." Hot tears burned my eyes. Rage.

Pain.

Fear. Especially fear.

I'd finally started to feel safe, to think that I could somehow be free from Hayes and all the ways he'd tortured me and controlled me over the years, but now I knew it was nothing but a pipe dream.

"I'm so sorry you've gotten dragged into all of this," I said. "I should never have involved you."

"Don't be," Ethan bit off. "I'm glad you involved me. I want to be involved."

I shot my gaze over to meet his. Fierce. That was the only word that could possibly describe the expression staring back at me.

"But Carter shouldn't have to—"

"This is allowing me to teach my son what it means to be a real man," Ethan cut in. "To show him how we treat people. It's helping me to be the kind of example for him that I never had."

I shook my head, ready to tell him I'd pack my things and leave tonight. Not that I had a clue where I'd go. There had to be a women's shelter around here, though. Every city had them these days. I could go to a shelter and be far away from Ethan and Carter, so they could go back to their lives and forget all about the upheaval I'd brought them.

"Hayes is throwing a wrench into things," Ethan said. "That's all. But we're not going to let him win. We're not going to let him get away with this. We'll find some angle that we haven't thought of yet, stumble on evidence that's been eluding us. Something. But we're not going to give up. We're not throwing in the towel and letting him off."

My mind got stuck on the fact that Ethan had said *we*. Suddenly, I didn't feel alone. My mind latched onto it almost as much as my heart did.

His eyes bored into me, intense and almost pained, pleading with me. "I'll take care of you, Natalie. If you'll let me. Me and Carter, and even Snoopy. We'll take care of you."

A sob tore through me, vicious and agonizing in its efforts to break free, somehow even more painful when it got trapped in my chest.

In a flash, Ethan crossed the room. He sat beside me, the couch dipping beneath his weight so that I fell against him, and he drew me into his arms. "He can't hurt you," Ethan murmured, tucking my head beneath his chin. "He can't ever hurt you again. I'll make sure of it."

I was sorely tempted to believe Ethan's promises. But the truth was that Hayes didn't need to be near me to hurt me. He'd already done enough that even if he no longer existed, he could still hurt me.

Physical injuries could heal. Broken bones mended. Scars faded with time. The things he'd done to my heart, though? To my mind? How could a person ever come out on the other side of that kind of pain?

Despite the impossibility of ever coming out on the other side, I allowed myself to sink further into the façade of safety I felt in Ethan's arms. I wanted to burrow against him and pretend, just for a little while, that I could have a normal life, that a strong, protective man could keep me safe from all the dangers of the world, and that I could finally be free.

Ethan shifted my legs, drawing them across his lap and allowing me to burrow into his embrace. I rested my head against the broad expanse of muscles lining his chest, my fingers just skimming his abdomen. His powerful arms enveloped me.

If I closed my eyes, I could almost believe the illusion.

But if I left them closed too long, reality returned, along with the memories of all that Hayes had done.

Chapter Nineteen

Ethan

The news of my father's involvement in the case seemed to shake Natalie more than I'd been expecting. Sure, she let me draw her into my arms and hold her, but at the same time, it felt as if she were closing off some part of herself, stacking more bricks onto her protective wall. I'd hoped that we were finally starting to tear that wall down, one painstaking piece at a time, and that we were making progress toward eliminating it entirely. But instead, we were once again moving in the opposite direction.

Carter's gleeful shouts and Snoopy's excited barks out back were such a sharp contrast to the heavy weight settling between us inside. But at the same time, they were proof that, with the right care, anyone could live a good life.

That damn dog had been left on the side of the road to suffocate and die, but I'd never known a pup so loyal and loving before. He'd always be undersized because of the malnourishment he suffered before I had him, but that didn't prevent him from opening up his heart to every human he came into contact with.

Carter was constantly being shuttled back and forth between my home and Kinsey's, but he *knew* we both loved him, and he was the sweetest fucking kid I'd ever been around. The way he treated Natalie was the only evidence required to see what a big heart he had.

But kids and animals healed faster than adults. They were more forgiving. They soaked up love and affection, letting it fill them up instead of trying to fight it off, thinking they didn't deserve it. They tended to assume the best of people instead of expecting the worst.

I needed to convince Natalie that I could keep her safe, but how could I do that when, with every day that passed, I felt less certain of it myself?

She snuggled against me, trying to get closer, so I cautiously tightened my arms around her. I wanted her to feel safe and protected but not trapped. It was probably a very fine line between the two extremes.

"How did I end up like this?" Her lips barely brushed the side of my neck as she spoke, and her eyelashes fluttered softly against my skin just before a hot tear dripped to my chest. "I was supposed to be too smart for this. I was in the top ten of my high school class. Top ten students, not just the top ten percent, even. I had scholarship offers from four different universities, but I turned them all down because Hayes wanted me with him wherever he ended up playing hockey. He didn't want me to go to college. I used to be smart. How did I end up so stupid?"

"You're not stupid."

"I have to be."

"Look at me," I said, and I tipped up her chin until she met my eyes. "You're *not* stupid. Maybe he wanted you to think you are, but that was all him. Because he felt the need to control you, probably because he felt out of control himself. That's all it was. But it doesn't make you stupid."

"I feel like such an idiot," she said, her eyes swimming.

"Please don't call yourself that. Not in front of me."

I wanted to kiss her tears away, but I'd already gone further than I should have by dragging her into my lap. Instead, I forced myself to keep my hands where they were, my lips far away from hers.

"I don't deserve you, Ethan," she said. "I don't know what I've done to have you in my life, but—"

"You deserve so much better than me."

She shook her head. "There's no such thing. There is no one better than you."

"You're wrong."

"Not about this. Not for me."

Everything in my chest clenched at her words and the sincerity in her eyes. I wanted to kiss her more than I wanted to breathe, but I'd meant what I'd said before—if anything was going to happen between us, she was going to have to initiate it. In her own time, when she was ready, and not a moment before. I'd broken part of that vow by holding her, but I wouldn't do more than that.

And however much I hoped she was ready, that she'd make her move now, I knew it was too soon.

After a long, electrically-charged moment, Carter and Snoopy interrupted us by slamming open the back door and racing inside, both of them sopping wet.

"I think it's gonna rain!" Carter shouted as Natalie squirmed to get off my lap, her cheeks pink. But was it a blush or something else?

"You sure about that?" I replied, reluctantly helping her shift over.

"There's a lotta clouds."

Sure enough, some more dark storm clouds had rolled in. I checked the weather app on my phone, and it said we might actually get a good soak. About fucking time.

"We should go sit outside in it," Natalie suggested.

"I'm gonna do a rain dance," Carter said, racing up the stairs.

"Why are you going upstairs?" I called after him, but he and Snoopy were already gone. Seconds later, the door to Carter's room slammed closed.

"A rain dance?" Natalie repeated, laughing softly.

"No idea. I guess we'll both see in a minute." But with any luck, it would work.

Chapter Twenty

Natalie

When Carter and Snoopy rushed back down the stairs, both Ethan and I burst into uncontrollable laughter.

Carter had donned a Thunderbirds sweater that fell to his knees and had sleeves so long he might trip on them, a bright orange toy hardhat that nearly covered his eyes, a pair of school-bus-yellow scuba fins, neon blue goggles, and lime-green swim trunks we could barely make out beneath the sweater. The clashing colors were almost blinding, and he had a fake peacock feather sticking up from the hardhat. No telling where he'd found that last bit, but it certainly added a touch of flair to the ensemble. He'd tied a Batman cape around Snoopy's neck, which was draped across his back like a doggie poncho. The only thing missing was a hat of some sort for the dog.

"What's all that for?" Ethan asked once he'd regained his composure.

Carter rolled his eyes. "I already *told* you. I'm gonna do a rain dance." There was so much *duh* in his tone he was practically dripping with it. Clearly, we were silly grownups who didn't know anything about rain dances.

"Got it," Ethan said, still laughing. "Since you're in your swim trunks, how about we see if we can go visit Drew and Ravyn? Then you two can get in the pool."

That sounded dangerous to me. "If there's lightning…"

"We'll keep an eye on things," Ethan said. But he was already taking out his phone and shooting off a text to his teammate. "You have anything you can swim in? It's plenty hot enough still. Or do you have to keep the tattoo dry?"

"I bet Ravyn and I can figure something out," I said. To be honest, I wouldn't mind getting back in the pool for a while, as long as I didn't get electrocuted. And whether I could get in the pool or not, at least Ravyn would be there to remind me about the rules.

Drew responded to Ethan's text almost immediately, inviting us all over. In no time, the four of us were piling into Ethan's car and on our way to his teammate's house.

They only lived about five minutes away, and there wasn't any traffic to speak of tonight. Maybe everyone else in Tulsa had the same idea we did—sit around and pray for a good storm with plenty of rain.

Carter rushed up to the front door before Ethan had even shut off the engine. Snoopy raced behind him, barking, which alerted Drew and Ravyn of our arrival even before Carter had managed to ring the bell. They opened the door and let the boy and his dog rush through the house and straight out back without even slowing down to say hello. Ethan and I followed a bit more slowly, me carefully walking and using the crutches for balance, Ethan behind me as if to catch me in case I fell.

"No getting in the pool for two weeks," Ravyn said when we reached the porch. "Not unless you cover that sucker so well none of the chlorine can possibly get through it." Apparently, I didn't even need to bother asking—she'd anticipated my question and had her answer ready to go. "At least not if you want to keep your tattoo looking good. But you can sit by the water and dip your toes in, or else I can put a hardcore bandage on it for you—something that'll keep all the chlorine out, no matter how deep you go."

"Trust me, dipping my toes in is more than good enough for me right now."

"Dip your toes in?" Ethan said quietly, so no one else would hear. "So I guess your tattoo isn't on your foot."

I laughed. "I still haven't shown you, have I?" But of course, I knew I hadn't shown him yet. I wanted the moment to be right. It felt like such a part of me already, something very personal and private.

Ethan winked and slipped past me, probably in a hurry to get out back so he could keep an eye on Carter and Snoopy. Drew followed them, leaving Ravyn and me alone.

"No problems with it?" she asked as we trailed behind them at my pace.

"Nothing but crazy itching."

"Remember what I told you. Don't scratch it. Just put more lotion or cream on it."

"Regular lotion isn't enough."

"Maybe use some bag balm, then."

"Bag balm?" I'd never heard of it before.

"They use it on lactating cows. It's seriously the best stuff out there. I've got some I can send home with you. It'll get better soon." She stopped in the middle of the living room. "Want to change into something to sit out there? Drew's getting burgers ready to go on the grill. I told him he's crazy, because they're going to get rained out. Either that or we still won't get any rain, and a spark from the grill will light the grass on fire, and then the whole neighborhood will go up in flames. But he's willfully ignoring me."

I'd never heard her speak so much at once before, but I was glad she was the one doing the talking. It saved me the effort of sifting through the surprises of the day to come up with small talk. In all honesty, I didn't think I was capable of it right now. Not after everything Ethan had told me. I was doing well just to be standing upright and not cowering somewhere, waiting for the sky to fall.

Since it'd been so hot all day, I was already wearing a tank top and a pair of shorts. That seemed plenty good enough for this, so I shook my head. "I'm fine like this. I'll just dip my toes in, like you said. No reason to change, and that won't put my tattoo at risk from the chlorine."

"Well, I'm putting on a swimsuit because it's hot as Hades out there. If this storm doesn't bring us some rain, the least it could do is bring in a cold front. I'm tired of ninety-degree-plus weather!"

I laughed, and she scurried off to change clothes.

By the time I made it outside to join the guys, Carter and Snoopy were already doing their rain dance. That little boy was jumping around in circles, whooping and hollering a war chant the fans sometimes shouted at T-Birds home games, only he'd changed the words. The only thing I could make out was, "We need more rain, lots of wet rain, soaking wet rain. Give us all your rain!" Snoopy kept barking and jumping with him, excited to be joining in the fun even if he had no idea what was going on.

"If that doesn't work, nothing will," Drew said, shaking his head. He walked over to the grill and threw the burgers on it.

I joined Ravyn at the table beneath the umbrella and helped her prepare the burger fixings, and Ethan stood with his teammate by the grill, seemingly keeping one eye on the rain dancers and the other on the sky.

I took a look at the sky, as well. Those clouds rolling in from the west looked ominous and promising, all at once. But if we had another electrical storm in store for us, sitting out by the pool might not be the brightest idea. And getting in the water would be even stupider.

"Do you think we'll get thunder and lightning?" I asked Ravyn as I reached for another tomato to slice. I hadn't been in Oklahoma all that long, so I still hadn't adjusted to the change in weather patterns. I just knew it was a lot different than things up in Michigan.

"No telling, this time of year. But if we do, we'll have to drag everyone away from the pool."

"Exactly what I was thinking."

"Weatherman's calling for rain," Drew called loud enough we could hear it. "Didn't say anything about storms."

"How much rain, though?" Ravyn asked.

"No matter how much we get, it won't be

enough," Ethan put in. He stripped his shirt over his head, and my belly fluttered at the sight of the muscles flexing in his back and shoulders. He tossed the shirt onto the ground near my feet.

I tried not to gawk, but honestly, Ethan was one impeccable specimen. With his back to me so he could keep an eye on Carter and Snoopy, I had an excellent view of broad shoulders leading down to a narrow waist.

"Just you wait," Ravyn said. She winked at me when I turned my head. She must have seen me gawking. "Once it really gets going, we're going to need an ark to get anywhere."

"Only because the ground's so hard it can't sink in fast enough," Drew said. "They had rain like that down in parts of Texas last fall. That was why they had so many floods around Houston and whatnot."

"Oh, like the one that killed that whole family?" Ravyn asked. "Their whole house floated away in the floods, and they were trapped inside."

"We're not going to float away," Drew reassured her.

"I just hope we get enough to get my hair wet," Ethan said.

Drew snort-laughed. "You've got a better chance of that than the rest of us, Bear. Since you're closer to the sky." But at the same moment as he flipped the burgers, something in the air changed.

It was the scent.

The air smelled wet and fresh, like rain, even though nothing was falling yet.

"I think we might actually get some," I said. "Do you guys smell that?"

"All I smell is burgers," Drew said.

But Ravyn turned her head away from the grill and sniffed. "Natalie's right. It smells like rain."

"Don't jinx it," her husband said, brandishing his burger flipper in our direction, and we both held up our hands to show we weren't doing anything. Not that there was anything we *could* do, other than pray.

Carter was spinning in circles so fast and chanting his rain-dance song so thoroughly that he wasn't paying attention to where his feet landed. One second, he was dancing at the edge of the pool; the next, he had fallen into the water with a massive belly flop.

Snoopy barked and followed him into the water.

And then, the heavens opened up with an almost torrential downpour of glorious, cool rain, falling in sheets. It was like nothing I'd never seen before.

We got plenty of rain back home in Michigan. We even got a good thunderstorm from time to time. But we'd never gotten anything like this before, not in as long as I could remember.

"It worked!" Carter spluttered, trying to stay afloat despite the components of his costume dragging him down, followed by the dog flailing all over him in the water.

Like the SuperDad he was, Ethan was at the edge of the pool in a flash. He didn't even need to get in— he just stretched out a long arm and plucked both the boy and the dog free from the water, setting them on the edge of the pool. "You'd better take most of that off if you're going to swim."

"But I can swim? Even though it's raining?"

"As long as we don't hear any thunder or see any lightning," Ethan agreed.

Drew quickly shut the cover over the grill while all

of that was going on, to shelter the burgers from the downpour. And Ravyn and I rushed to be sure all the food we'd been prepping was protected from the deluge.

But then we'd done all we could for our food.

I shucked off my brace to keep the liner from getting wet, and then we were out in it, all of us, letting the water soak us to the bone. I kept most of my weight on my crutches and my good leg since I wasn't wearing my protective boot, and surprisingly, I did all right that way.

Nothing could have kept me from going out in this rain, though, not even if it hurt.

The water felt amazing, cool and slick over my skin, like satin sheets on a hot summer night.

Ethan took a seat at the edge of the pool, letting his feet fall into the water, probably so he'd be close enough to make another quick rescue or to haul an uncooperative child or dog out in case of thunder or lightning.

But Ravyn and Drew were still trying to salvage dinner, and I felt guilty standing out in the rain while they were working, so I moved back under the umbrella to help.

Ravyn narrowed her eyes at me, then jerked her head in Ethan's direction.

"What?" I asked.

"Go. We've got this under control. If anyone deserves to enjoy a night sitting out in the rain with a man like that one, it's you."

The temptation combined with Ravyn's permission—or rather, *encouragement*—was all it took. Once I was behind Ethan, I lowered my crutches to the ground before lowering myself to my knees behind him, using his shoulders for support in case I slipped on the way down.

He tensed beneath my touch, his muscles all taut and ready to spring into action, and I could feel his heart hammering through his ribs.

"Ethan?"

He didn't answer.

He didn't need to.

Instead, he turned his head to the side, just as I slid my hands forward and brought my mouth to his, my chest pressed to his back. It only lasted a moment, soft as butterfly wings and light as a marshmallow, but it lit a fire inside me that no amount of rain would be able to quench.

When I backed away and looked in his eyes again, that fire became an inferno.

I'd never seen a man look at me in that way before, so full of heat and need and longing. But now I was ready for him to take over, to show me what he wanted, to tell me what he needed from me. I expected him to take control.

He didn't move a muscle.

"Was that okay?" I asked, suddenly unsure of myself.

"Fuck, yes," he ground out.

"You're not— I'm just— I don't know what you want."

He was still looking at me with the same hunger as before, which only confused me more. But he never removed his gaze from mine, holding steady despite the buckets of rain falling over us. "I want you," he finally said, and those butterfly wings started fluttering their way down somewhere near the vicinity of my heart. "I want anything you want to do.

Anything you're ready for. Anything you can give me. Anything you need me to give to you. I want it all."

I was crying again, but the rain washed away my tears, so maybe he didn't see them before I leaned in and pressed my lips to his again. But there was no way he missed the sob that tore through me. He swallowed it with his kiss, somehow taking away a bit of the pain from my heart, leaving behind only those fluttery butterfly wings as evidence it had ever been there at all.

Chapter Twenty-One

Natalie

When we returned to Ethan's house a couple of hours later, we were all still wet and soggy from the rain and the pool, not to mention the heat. The moment we were inside, I shivered uncontrollably because the air conditioning was still blaring at full blast.

"Straight to the bathroom," Ethan said to Carter, who was already racing up the stairs. "Take off all the wet stuff and leave it on the floor for me, then get in the tub."

"It's too cold to take off my clothes!"

"That's why you're getting in the tub, wise guy. The water'll warm you up faster than anything else will." Ethan snagged Snoopy before he could follow his boy up the stairs, hauling the dog into the kitchen, where he'd already piled a bunch of towels. He started drying Snoopy in there, probably to contain as much of the water as possible to a minimal number of rooms.

"Do you need any help?" he asked me, almost

casually, but there couldn't be anything nonchalant about that question after the handful of kisses we'd shared out by the pool.

"No, I can manage," I said, but everything in me was burning to ask him for assistance. I shouldn't do that, though, because he had Carter, Snoopy, and himself to deal with.

He didn't need to worry about me, too.

"Get in the shower to warm up," he said.

"I will," I replied. But I'd rather get in his arms to warm up. Something told me Ethan had more than enough body heat to spare. I headed off to grab some dry clothes from my drawers before making my way into the bathroom.

"Leave your clothes on the floor in your room. I'll come grab them once the water's running and the door's closed."

If it weren't for the fact that I was freezing, I might have stood there and argued that I could deal with my own clothes once I got out. But there wasn't any point in keeping mine separate from his and Carter's, and I couldn't stop shivering, so I needed to get into the warm water, pronto.

The moment the water sprayed down over me, I couldn't stop the indulgent groan from falling from my lips. My fingers and toes tingled from the sharp juxtaposition of temperatures, until finally my outside matched my inside.

I stayed under the falling water longer than I should have, but it felt too good to climb out right away. I couldn't indulge too long, though, because Carter needed enough warm water for his bath, and Ethan would need to warm up, too. I shut it off before I was ready for the shower to end, determined not to be too greedy.

I wrapped a thick towel around my body and headed back into my bedroom, but I nearly bumped headfirst into Ethan. He was on his way out, carrying my wet things.

"Sorry," we both said at the same time.

"I put a robe in the dryer for you." Ethan nodded his head, indicating a scrap of folded red terrycloth on the foot of my bed. "To warm it up," he added. "I thought I could get it in here before you were done."

"Thank you. I wanted to hurry so I could leave you some hot water," I explained.

"You didn't need to do that. But thank you," he replied.

And then we both stood there awkwardly, neither moving but unsure what to say. Everything we *did* say made us sound like broken records.

"I thought—" I started, but then I cut myself off, because I wasn't sure how to proceed. "You wanted to see my tattoo," I finally finished. "Maybe I could...show you. If you still want to see it."

"I did. I do."

But he was carrying my wet clothes and still wearing some of his own, dripping water all over the floor. He hadn't had a chance to clean off and warm up yet.

I was an idiot for suggesting it now. "I'm sorry," I said. "Bad timing."

"Later. After I get Snoopy dry and Carter in bed."

"And you need to dry off and warm up, yourself, too."

"I do." He passed his gaze over me, as if taking a mental inventory of everything, scanning to see if I'd hurt myself or gotten sick from being wet and cold, or any number of other things.

But maybe it wasn't that at all. Maybe he was looking at me in a different manner altogether, and I was just having difficulty accepting it even if it was the very thing I wanted.

Regardless, his plan seemed altogether more reasonable, so I nodded and slipped past him into my bedroom, gently closing the door behind me.

The warm bathrobe was absolute perfection. I wrapped myself in it and sank onto the mattress to warm up for a few minutes. But those few minutes were too exquisite and far too indulgent for me to want them to end. It would be entirely too easy to stay exactly like this for hours if I allowed myself.

But I couldn't do that, even if the thought was tempting. I had to start being responsible for myself again at some point. I put on my brace, in an effort to act like an adult and so I wouldn't forget about it and accidentally hurt myself, but then I lay back against the pillows and halfway dozed off. Before I was ready, Ethan was knocking on my door and I still hadn't moved a muscle.

"Come in," I called, tugging on the robe to be sure I was covered.

He poked his head through and raised a brow. "Thought you would've gotten into your pj's by now." While he hadn't had a chance to shower yet, he'd changed into dry clothes.

"Seemed like too much effort," I joked. I sat up and patted the mattress in invitation. "But I haven't rebandaged the tattoo yet, so now's a good time for you to see it. I need to put some of that stuff on it that Ravyn sent home with me, anyway."

"I think that's still out in the car. I can go get it for

you."

"Not yet," I said. I reached out a hand to stop him.

He cautiously took my hand, and the heat was enough to set my body on fire. But finally, he sat beside me.

The entire bed seemed to dip under his weight, and I almost toppled over onto him. I put my hands out to catch myself, and they landed on his chest and biceps. His muscles almost rippled beneath my touch. He still smelled like the rain, only it had combined with his natural scent to become something heady and addictive. Something I wanted to melt against.

"Sorry," I said.

But he just helped me straighten myself up again, his massive hand lingering on my forearm before he seemed sure I could sit up on my own. "Don't be," he murmured. "I'm not."

I raised a brow in question.

"Gave me an excuse to touch you without coming across like a jackass or a creeper."

"You don't need an excuse to touch me."

He closed his eyes, and I could almost feel his inaudible groan vibrating the mattress. "I didn't come in here to touch you," he said quietly.

"I know you didn't."

"You're killing me."

"But would you, though?" I asked, despite my hesitance to put the suggestion out there. Everything had been so good between us. I didn't want to screw that up, but I'd already initiated a change in our relationship tonight when I'd kissed him.

We couldn't go back in time. I didn't *want* to go back, either. I wanted to keep exploring this, wherever it took us, whatever it meant.

He let out an almost pained sound, his eyes still closed.

"When I'm ready," I clarified. I reached for his hand and threaded my fingers through his, and he finally looked at me again, dark and serious and tortured. "Not right now. Not right away. But would you touch me if I asked you to?"

"I'd do anything you asked of me."

I had to bite my lower lip to stop myself from asking him for too much too soon. Because, while I might be ready for a few kisses, and I might *want* to feel his strong hands on my skin, I knew I needed more time to heal.

Not just physically—emotionally.

As part of my outpatient rehab, they'd started sending me to a support group and some private counseling to help me process the emotional aspects of my trauma. I'd only scratched the surface of all the internal healing I needed to do. At the same time, I recognized that in order to truly come to terms with everything I'd been through, I would have to gather up the courage to move forward.

This was part of my recovery. *Ethan* was part of my recovery. So were Carter and Snoopy, and all the WAGs who'd stood by my side.

But trusting a man, accepting his touch and moving into a physical, emotional relationship again—that was one more step I needed to take if I ever wanted to be free of Hayes. And I wanted that more than I could say, even though I knew it wouldn't happen overnight. Someday. With a lot of work and any amount of luck, it might be someday soon.

But however soon or distant that aspect of my

healing might be, I needed time.

Ethan seemed willing to give me all that I required.

The only problem was, I wasn't sure I'd be so willing to wait.

I bit my lower lip and looked down at my lap to avoid the combination of heat and gentleness in his stare, because I wasn't sure what to do with them. But then I untied the belt of the robe and cautiously opened it so that he could see the ink on my lower abdomen, just above my left hip, cautiously keeping my private bits covered. "It's still healing, but—"

"It's gorgeous," Ethan cut in. "It's perfect." He trailed a single finger along the curve of my hip, as if tracing the pattern even though he wasn't close enough to make contact with the design itself.

That slight connection made every nerve ending in my body go haywire.

I wanted more.

The texture of his eyes turned dark and needy, matching the ache building inside me.

"Ethan?" I said, both hesitant and demanding.

His eyes shot up to meet mine, his finger still resting gently just inside the curve of my hipbone.

"Will you kiss me?"

He answered with strong hands gently capturing the sides of my face, skilled fingers diving into my still-damp hair, and hungry lips softly moving cautiously over mine. I reached up and grabbed hold of his wrists to brace myself, my breath floating away as readily as my heart.

Just when I felt I might explode from wanting more, he slid his tongue along the crease of my lips, requesting entry. I opened and welcomed him in with a whimper of need, leaning back against the pillows and dragging him with me until his large body almost completely covered mine.

I wanted that contact, his weight pressing me into the mattress, but he held himself above me, teeth and lips and tongue almost our only contact.

"Touch me," I pleaded, breaking away for air.

"You have no idea how much I want to," he said, but I was pretty sure he was wrong about that. I had every idea if he felt anything like I did right now. But still, he wouldn't put his hands on me.

I'd never desired anything more than the sensation of those big hands on my body. I knew he'd be gentle. I knew he'd be everything Hayes wasn't.

"Please, Ethan."

I slid one of my hands down his powerful arm, trying to guide his hand to where I wanted it, but he wouldn't budge.

"This is too fast," he said. "Too soon. You're not ready."

And even though I knew he was right, even though rushing into any sort of a physical relationship was the last thing on earth I should be doing, I didn't want to believe it.

"You said you'd give me anything I asked you for," I reminded him, "as long as it was something you could give me. You said it had to start with me. Well, I'm trying to start it. I'm trying to tell you what I want. What I need. I need you," I finished, somehow getting it all out without my words turning into a strangled sob.

Ethan resettled his weight on the bed, his hands still locked in my hair, and he gently nudged me until I rolled over beside him, the length of his body warming mine. He pressed a soft kiss to my lips, to the tip of my nose, to the bridge of my forehead between my eyebrows. "It was the truth then, and it's still true now," he finally said. "I'll give you anything I can if it's in my power to give it to you. And I can't even begin to tell you how bad I want you—to touch you, to be with you, to show you what it ought to be like when you're with a decent man. But I'm begging you to slow down."

"I don't want to slow down."

"I know you don't. But I want to build something that can last with you. And I need to be sure you're ready for that."

Even though one part of me deflated in frustration, another part of me melted inside.

Ethan was exactly what I needed. Even if he was making me crazy with wanting him.

Chapter Twenty-Two

Ethan

Keeping my hands to myself around Natalie, the way I'd promised I'd do, might actually kill me. Especially now that Carter was on a flight back home to be with his mother, so Snoopy was the only potential road block remaining.

Other than my own conscience, at least. Which meant that my conscience was the only road block, because Snoopy didn't want to get between us unless it meant getting snuggles from both of us at once. It would be way too easy to just close a door and leave Snoopy on the other side of it.

And since I now knew that Natalie wanted to take things between us to another level, possibly even as much as I did, I wasn't sure how long I'd be able to hold out. Yes, I knew she needed more time. She recognized it, too, if she slowed down for long enough to think things through.

She had started speaking with a trauma therapist and a sexual assault counselor in her biweekly rehab sessions at the hospital, at least, so she had other people who could help her recognize that she might be getting in over her head. But even with counseling and therapy, it was still so soon for Natalie to be thinking about jumping into a physical relationship with anyone.

I was afraid she was just walking into the first open arms she could find, and they happened to be mine.

Now, if she needed me to be her rebound, I'd do it in a heartbeat—I'd be whatever she wanted me to be. But if that was what happened between us, if I was nothing more than the guy she felt safe enough with to get her mojo back, it'd be hell on me when she moved on.

Because I wanted this to be *more*. I was falling for her, and I was falling hard.

Maybe the guys were right and I was just a big softie, someone who picked up random strays and took them home with me.

I'd done it with Snoopy, after all. He and I were kindred spirits.

And in a way, Natalie and I were kindred spirits, too. I didn't think this connection I felt with her was solely because I'd been through an experience similar to what she'd been through, though. There was something bigger between the two of us. Something that ran deeper than the surface. We both felt it, and that had to be what had drawn her to seek out a physical component to our relationship.

If I ended up with a broken heart, so be it. I was an adult; I could take it. After all I'd been through, there wasn't a doubt in my mind that I could deal with whatever life threw at me. I was strong enough that I could take a metaphorical beating easily as well as I could take a physical one, and still get up and move on with my life.

It'd rip me to shreds for a while if Natalie wanted to move on—maybe a very long while—but I'd survive it.

The problem was, I didn't *want* to survive it. Not if it meant watching Natalie walk away, once the danger had been dealt with, once she had healed both physically and emotionally.

It might be more than I cared to handle. I'd do it, though.

She could use me for whatever she needed me for, and then I'd let her go. I had to, or I'd be no better than Lennon and his friends, no better than my own father. So even if it ripped out my heart to let her walk away, I'd do it.

With even a smidge of luck, I wouldn't have to face that fear.

I just had to stand my ground about not jumping into bed with her so soon. I wasn't sure how I could be certain when she was ready, but I knew it wasn't now.

We had a game tonight against the Red Wings. I'd already taken my pregame nap and was starting to get ready to head up to the arena when my phone buzzed with a text message.

> Carter: *Mrs. K said play good 2nite but not too good cuz the Wings need to do better this year.*

Mrs. Kuchner, otherwise known as Mrs. K, was Carter's second-grade teacher this year. I chuckled to myself and shot off a response.

Me: *Tell Mrs. K that the Wings can survive a loss this early in the season. We're going to try to win.*

Carter: *She said you can beat every1 else, just not the Wings.*

Me: *I can make no promises.*

Carter: *Just let Larkin score a goal, kay? He's her favrite.*

Me: *Not sure Hunter will agree to that, but I'll see what I can do.*

He seemed to find that answer acceptable, because he let it drop. But I had no intention of asking Hunter to let in any goals, regardless of who was shooting them.

Natalie was just coming back from rehab when I headed out into the living room. She had Tallie and Harper accompanying her. Harper ran straight over to Snoopy and hugged him around the neck. Good thing that dog loved being loved. He licked her face and they collapsed together onto the floor to roll around; she giggled and he barked like a loon.

Tallie shot her eyes skyward and shook her head.

"Maybe you should get her a puppy of her own," I suggested.

"Hunter wants to get her a baby brother or baby sister of her own. I think we'll start there."

"Dogs are easier than kids," I pointed out.

"True. But kids eventually deal with their own poop. Dogs just like to eat it."

"They don't all eat poop. Snoopy doesn't," I said, laughing, but my eyes were on Natalie.

She headed for the kitchen. When she came back a moment later, she set a bottle of water on the coffee table before propping her crutches against the side of the couch and settling in. "I would've offered to bring some for everyone, but I only have so many hands."

"We can all get our own," I replied.

With a shy nod, she took a moment to situate a pillow under her broken leg, then finally leaned back and relaxed.

"You need me for anything else right now?" Tallie asked.

"You've already done more than enough," Natalie said, shaking her head.

"London's picking you up later for the game?"

"Yes, I'm riding in with London and Erik."

"Then I'll see you tonight." Tallie extracted her daughter from climbing all over Snoopy, and a moment later, they were gone.

Snoopy watched out one of the front windows, barking when the car backed out of the driveway. Then he rushed back into the living room and jumped onto the couch next to Natalie, draping his head across her lap.

Damn if I didn't want to do exactly the same thing.

Especially when she stroked his head, almost absentmindedly. In no time, his tongue was lolling out of his mouth, and he rolled onto his back with his belly in the air, his tail wagging between his legs, and she automatically started rubbing his belly.

Yeah, I'd be toast if she stroked me that way. Lucky fucking dog.

"What?" she asked, dragging me out of my stupor.

I shot my gaze up to meet her eyes, finding an unanticipated heat there. "Just thinking about you touching me like that," I admitted.

"You're the one who said we have to wait."

"I know it. Doesn't mean I don't want it, though."

Natalie bit her lower lip and looked down at my kid's dog, putting even more effort into rubbing his belly. His back legs started doing an out-of-control shimmy-shake, which meant she'd found exactly the right spot.

"He'll love you forever if you keep rubbing him exactly like that for the next hour or two," I said.

"What about you?" Natalie's eyes flashed over to meet mine for just a second before focusing on Snoopy again. "Would you love me forever if I rubbed you a certain way?"

She didn't need to rub me for that to happen.

. . . . . .

To my frustration, Mrs. K got her wish two times over by halfway through the third period. Larkin and his linemates were already spilling over the boards again; he was on the hunt for a hat trick.

Prince and I needed to get off the ice for a line change, but the Wings had us trapped in our own defensive zone. Every time we thought we were going to clear out the puck for long enough to dive over the boards and get some fresh legs on the ice, the Wings' D somehow got it past our forwards and back into our defensive zone before even a single one of my teammates could get off for a change.

Larkin skated straight for the net, but one of his linemates had the puck and headed for the corner with it. Prince followed that guy, trying to knock the puck free, so I stayed in front of Hunter at the net, doing everything I legally could to get Larkin away from my goaltender.

No matter how many times I shoved his body, the fucker kept coming back like an annoying gnat. I pushed him hard in the back, finally getting him to move a few inches away from my goaltender's crease.

He shifted to the side, calling me a few choice words.

I whacked at his ankles with the blade of my stick.

He glanced over to see where the ref was before jabbing backwards with his elbow to get me off him.

They finally cleared the puck out of the corner, but the Wings controlled it, so we were still stuck.

The Wings' defensemen passed it from point to point, setting up for a slapshot.

It flew toward the mass of bodies that was Larkin, Hunter, and me.

Larkin just got the toe of his blade on the puck before I got my stick in the way, angling the puck away. Hunter got his glove on it just enough that the puck clanged off his pipe and squirted back out into the pile of bodies now converging on his crease.

I managed to trip and make it look accidental, taking Larkin down beneath me. Sometimes it paid to be big. No call on the play, thank fuck, and Frisky—otherwise known as Viktor Frisk, our Swedish top-line center—managed to get past all the Wings on the ice and corral the puck to prevent an icing call on the play.

I skated off the ice and chugged some water while the coaches shouted contradictory orders at us. Prince rolled his eyes at me when they headed down the line to yell at someone else. He didn't need to say anything; his eyes said it all.

"Exactly," I muttered.

The clock and the heat were the only things working in our favor right now. The Wings players weren't accustomed to playing in the kind of temperatures we'd been dealing with, and it was starting to take its toll on them. They were looking sluggish, and they weren't getting as much oomph on their shots as they had earlier in the night.

On our next couple of shifts together, Prince and I did a better job of keeping the play to the outside, so Hunter had a good view of the puck at all times. He made a couple of spectacular diving saves, and then I managed to skate the puck down to the other end of the ice.

I passed it off to Prince, who had a clear lane to the Wings' net and one of our forwards streaking into position to tip in his shot. He wound up for a slapper and somehow got it through all the bodies coming together without needing any assistance. It was his goal—no doubt about it. Our goal light went off and the horn sounded, and then the arena erupted into a tribal war chant.

"Fucking right," I said, slapping him on the back of the shoulder while the rest of our teammates converged to dogpile on top of him.

We were still losing the game, and Larkin might still come away with a fucking hat trick if we weren't careful—but we weren't going to be shut out tonight.

One thing at a time.

......

Before it was all said and done, Prince had scored again, tying the game to make it interesting.

Neither he nor Larkin had come away with a hat

trick, but the Wings had managed to win it all in overtime on a sneaky Nyquist backhander that had slipped past Hunter on a breakaway. But Prince had come insanely close to scoring a third goal with only seconds to spare in the third period, which would have made him the first player in the history of the Thunderbirds franchise to accomplish such a feat.

Because of that, all the reporters in the arena wanted a piece of him—which was essentially his worst nightmare.

I'd already finished showering and dressing after the game, but he still had a swarm of cameras surrounding his stall—many of them from the regular Detroit sports press. Since my stall was near his, I listened in so I could lend him a hand if necessary.

"What'd you think of the way your teammates kept getting you the puck there at the end of regulation?" one of them asked.

Prince shrugged and took a moment. "Thought they wanted to help."

Short and sweet—that was how he usually kept his responses.

"When Mrazek went down with only about twenty seconds left in the game, what were you thinking?" another asked.

"Th-thought shoot hard."

"That's it?" the same guy asked with a smirk in his tone. "Shoot hard?"

A few of the others surrounding Prince laughed. Fuckers.

"Yeah. Shoot hard."

I dragged a towel over my wet hair, listening intently. Most people didn't know that the reason Prince didn't tend to talk much was because he had a bit of a stutter. And frankly, I didn't *know* it; I had always just assumed it, which, admittedly, was probably not the best way to get my information. But he seemed to be growing more and more agitated, and that wasn't likely to help if my assumptions were correct.

Then some jackass I'd never seen before spoke up. "Travis, there's been a lot of talk around the league about the Thunderbirds name. What do you think about your team being named after one of the native tribes in Oklahoma? Isn't it degrading and demeaning? Should there be a call for the name to be changed?"

That did it. I wasn't going to stand there and listen to these sons of bitches for one second longer. I shoved my way in and stood next to my teammate, who was blinking in shock over the question, and I crossed my arms in an intimidating stance.

"First off, who wants to know what we think about the team name?" I bit off.

A couple of the reporters snickered and pointed at one guy near the front of the pack.

"You?" I asked, nodding toward the one they'd indicated.

I recognized him from growing up in Michigan. He'd been covering the Red Wings for a long time for one of the local papers. I'd always thought he was an ass, but this confirmed it.

He gave me a sheepish look, but he nodded. "I just thought you boys might have something to say about denigrating a people by making a mockery of them."

"Yeah, so here's a clue for you. Thunderbirds aren't a people. They're not a tribe. They're not a nation or whatever. They're a symbol, or maybe a god or some other sort of deity, depending on who you ask. But they're not a people, all right? So do your research before you go on the attack next time. And furthermore, you might try looking into what the Supreme Court has to say about team names like the Seminoles, the Indians, the Red Skins, and whatnot. There's been a ruling. A recent one, even. They say it's fine. But whether the Supreme Court agrees with it or not, an athlete plays for the team that signs him—end of story. Fucking idiot," I finished under my breath, but it was loud enough that Prince shot a look over at me and had to fight to keep from laughing.

Which meant it was loud enough for all the microphones around me to pick up.

Which meant I might be facing a fine with the league.

And probably with the team, too. Mrs. Jernigan wouldn't be too happy about that one, at the very least. I doubted ponying up a fine for the team's swear jar would be enough to mollify her this time.

It didn't matter that almost everyone in the room was laughing. I'd stepped over the line. That much was evident by the reporter's red face of fury staring back at me through the sea of faces.

"Funny," the guy said. "Really funny, especially coming from a guy who likes to throw around baseless accusations of assault. Did you know your father's getting involved in the case involving your teammate?"

"Former teammate," I bit off.

"Mr. Lennon's been wrongly suspended. I'm sure the suspension will be lifted once the team and the league are aware of the truth and all of this has been cleared up, which your father is helping to do. But he might just choose to sue you after that—defamation of character or something."

I bit my tongue because otherwise I might have bitten the guy's head off then and there. But that wouldn't help anything. Especially not with every other reporter suddenly leaning in, hoping to catch every little word they could.

"Did any of the rest of you guys have any questions for the Prince, here?" I asked, trying to deflect the attention off myself and put it back on my teammate, who'd been the only one on our side to score. He deserved to see a bit of the limelight after the night he'd had. And this was supposed to be about hockey, not about me and my father and Hayes Fucking Lennon.

One of them was quick to rescue me. "How'd it feel to have your first two-goal game in the National Hockey League?" a reporter near the back of the pack asked, and I dipped my head and left them to it. Prince could handle himself well enough from here.

When I got back to my stall, Spurs was waiting for me.

"The fuck were you thinking?" he bit off.

I shrugged. "Guess I wasn't."

"That much is clear. Gary's already on a call with the league."

Gary Asher was the team's general manager.

"Will I be suspended?"

"Definitely fined. I don't think the league can do more than that, according to the current Collective Bargaining Agreement—depends on what they decide to call it, possibly—but you're getting a fine no matter what. You can't spout off like that in front of reporters."

I nodded. I could accept that.

"The team'll fine you, too," he added.

"Mrs. J will insist on it, even if you weren't going to already."

Spurs chuckled. "That she will." But then he dropped his voice and leaned in conspiratorially. "Off the record, I would have had a hard time not decking the guy, so you did well just to curse at him. But don't do it again."

"Noted," I said, and I went back to changing my clothes.

He left, heading over to listen in on the rest of the Q&A session.

A few minutes later, Prince was finally relieved from talking to the press. He shuffled over to his stall, tucking his long hair behind his ear since it kept falling forward into his face. "Thanks," he said quietly.

I shrugged. "Nothing to thank me for. He's an ass and an idiot. I pointed it out. End of story."

"But y-you didn't h-have to—" Prince cut himself off, and he took a moment to collect his thoughts. "Just thanks," he finally finished, speaking slowly and staring down at the gear he was taking off.

I nodded and slapped him on the shoulder. Something told me the guy could use a hug, but he wouldn't take it well if I drew him in for a bro hug in the middle of the locker room—especially not with all the cameras and reporters still lurking. A shoulder slap would have to do for the time being.

But now, I wanted to get out of there so I could collect Natalie and head back to the house. We hadn't spoken since she'd talked about rubbing me in a certain way and wondering if I'd love her forever. I hadn't given her an answer then.

Honestly, I wasn't sure she was ready for my answer. Lord knew I wasn't. But the truth was, I might already be in love with her, and it had nothing to do with her touching me physically.

She'd touched me deeper than that, somewhere in the darkest, ugliest depths of my soul, where all the hurt and anger couldn't touch me, but somehow her goodness and light made its way through the darkness. And there's no going back once something like that happens. Not that I wanted to go back.

I was a goner when it came to Natalie.

A lost cause.

Toast.

And I was perfectly okay with that.

Chapter Twenty-Three

Natalie

Ethan was in an odd mood on the way back to his house after the game. Another big storm was blowing in, one that seemingly matched his demeanor—ominous clouds with flashes of electricity, a dark promise of more to come.

But Ethan didn't seem angry, or at least not angry with me. It was more that he'd closed off a part of himself, and he didn't want to grant me access to it. Or rather, to *him*.

I had no right to want access to any part of him, and he'd already given me more than I could have hoped for. I knew I shouldn't think too much of it…but his disposition ate away at me, nonetheless, like a cat slowly but doggedly gnawing at its prey.

"Got a Thundershirt for Snoopy," he said, finally breaking the stilted silence once we were a couple of blocks away from his house.

"A Thundershirt?"

"It's supposed to help keep animals calm during storms or for other things that upset them. Vet visits.

Fireworks. Strangers coming over. Any sort of loud noises that bother them. Wraps around them and helps them feel secure or something. Guess tonight'll be a good night to test it out."

Even as he spoke, another streak of lightning ripped through the dark sky, followed close behind by a massive boom of thunder. Now that we'd finally gotten some rain, it seemed there would be no end to it. The skies seemed to have been saving it all up and now wanted to send us a deluge. Which was probably for the best—unless it came too fast and the ground couldn't soak up all the water in time, causing floods.

But there was a part of me that wished we could just get some rain without a storm, even if I liked the storms. A good, solid soak could work wonders on the earth and the soul, both.

Ethan turned in at his driveway. He'd barely put the car in park in the garage when the skies opened up with a fresh downpour.

Snoopy met us at the door, shaking and cowering at Ethan's feet while somehow simultaneously attempting to jump into his arms. I could understand the sentiment; I wanted to jump into Ethan's arms, too, but for an entirely different reason.

He bent down on the floor and secured a complicated gray piece of fabric around Snoopy, using a series of Velcro straps to tighten it in place. When he stood up again, the dog looked kind of silly, as though wearing a doggie version of a straightjacket, but the wild terror was gone from his eyes. He whimpered with the next roll of thunder, but he didn't panic. It was just an I-don't-like-this sort of whine, not an I'm-about-to-die one.

If only there were something like a Thundershirt

for me when it came to facing whatever wrenches Hayes tried to throw into my path. But maybe Ethan could be my Thundershirt against the storm my life had become. I didn't think he'd mind wrapping himself around me to calm my fears.

Once Snoopy was suited up, Ethan headed for the living room, with the dog following close behind him. I joined them and sat on the sofa, taking off my brace to let my skin breathe and putting the ankle of my broken leg on the coffee table with a pillow beneath it for cushioning. My leg was almost fully healed—I shouldn't need the brace much longer at all, and I certainly didn't need it at home. It was simply a precaution at this point. Ethan sat next to me. Snoopy jumped up on his other side, and their combined weight caused me to lean toward them.

Or so I told myself.

I probably could have fought the urge to roll into Ethan's arms, but I wasn't inclined to do anything of the sort. It was far more gratifying to feel the strength of Ethan's body alongside my own, the heavy weight of his frame grounding me to reality.

More tentative than I'd ever known him to be, Ethan settled an arm around me, tugging me against his side. His heat was just as seductive as his clean scent and the energy coursing through the air outside.

Forgetting all about trying to keep myself upright, I leaned in and reveled in the sense of security I found in his presence, the comfort I found in his strength.

There was just as much electricity crackling inside as there was outside. Ethan had to feel it, as powerful as it was. The very air we were breathing seemed alive, almost sizzling. We could fry an egg on it if we wanted to.

"We haven't really spent much time alone," I observed, cautiously easing my way into talking about all the things that remained unsaid between us.

He didn't respond for a moment. And then, "No, we haven't." Short and sweet, and incredibly quiet. Tentative, almost, even though there was typically nothing tentative about Ethan.

"There are usually doctors or nurses or some of the guys from the team around."

"Or Carter."

"Or Carter," I agreed.

"I feel safer when there's someone else with us."

That reaction made me blink with incomprehension. "Safer?"

He made a soft sound. "Because I won't be tempted to do things I shouldn't. Not if someone else is with us. But when we're alone..."

An uncomfortable and exciting tingle filled my chest. My pulse quickened, and my breaths fell heavy from my lips. "What sorts of things?"

He didn't respond, so I looked up and met his eyes. They were full of heat. "You know what sorts of things," he finally said.

Suddenly, my mouth was dry. I licked my lips to wet them, but it didn't do much other than draw his eye.

"I do," I said with as much confidence as I could put into those two tiny words. "And I also know I want those things. I want them as much as you do. Maybe even more. Because I need to know..."

But I couldn't finish the thought. I felt too raw to go there, even though Ethan was surely the safest man in the world for me to talk about these things with—the still-raw pieces of my soul. He was the only one I wanted to see those parts of me. The only one I felt safe enough with to expose the most broken shards, the shattered veneer of protection that had once existed around my heart.

"Need to know what?" Ethan asked a moment later, which provided me with just enough impetus to power through.

"I need to know what it's like when I want it."

"You're killing me." He clearly didn't need me to explain further.

"*You're* killing *me*," I repeated. "We both want it."

"I'm not going to rush you, Natalie. I won't push you."

"Maybe I want to push you and not the other way around. Maybe I want you to let me. Maybe I want to touch you. To taste you. To feel your hands on me. To put my hands on you."

"Maybe I want to give in," he rasped, but he looked like he wanted to take the words back.

There would be no taking those words back. Not on my watch.

"So give in," I replied. "Let me touch you."

He closed his eyes and let out the softest, most painfully erotic groan I'd ever heard.

Seizing the opportunity, I shifted my weight around and propped myself up on my knees, straddling his thighs.

"Natalie," he said on a strangled sigh, but I cut him off by kissing him.

It was a tentative kiss, at first—a gentle brush of my lips over his, a soft swipe of tongue. I wanted to test him out, and he let me, even if every taut muscle in his body said he wanted to do nothing of the sort.

But when I slid my tongue past his teeth, he groaned and opened for me, falling back against the couch cushions and bracing my hips with his powerful hands while our tongues tangled.

I ripped at his tie and got it free, then flung it over my shoulder before fumbling with the series of buttons closing his shirt and getting enough of them undone to free the hollow of his neck. As soon as it was available to me, I lowered my lips to that spot, kissing and licking him there until his Adam's apple bobbed seductively.

A crack of thunder sounded, and Snoopy whimpered and burrowed closer to us. Ethan groaned and picked me up, carrying me into my bedroom and kicking the door closed behind us. When he sat down on the edge of the bed, it was with me straddling his thighs, his hardness pulsing against the apex of my thighs with a seductive heat.

"Touch me," I begged, continuing my quest to free all the rippling muscles of his chest and abdomen, my voice harsh and raspy.

"How?" His hands clenched against my hips, as if he needed to brace himself. "Where? Tell me what you want."

"I want you." It was the only coherent thought I could form, the only words my brain could come up with.

"Show me," he said, his words almost inaudible over the frantic pounding of my heart.

I sat back, straddling his thighs, frustrated and frantic for more. But the heat in his expression soothed my battered nerves.

He reached for my hand with one of his own, guiding me to take his other wrist. "Show me what you want," he repeated, more strongly this time.

But other than *not Hayes*, I wasn't sure what I wanted.

I hesitated, my desire warring with my uncertainty and my insecurities.

Maybe I wasn't ready. Maybe I was rushing into Ethan's open, willing arms before I should. Maybe I was just using him to fulfill a need, to help me prove to myself that Hayes hadn't ruined me beyond repair, that I could handle being touched by a man as long as it wasn't Hayes.

Except...that wasn't entirely true. Because I wanted *Ethan*. I wanted all of him. Everything he could give me.

"We don't have to do this," Ethan said, breaking through the fog filling my thoughts. His eyes were filled with so much concern it felt like a sharp stab in my gut. "You don't have to—"

"I want this," I cut in. "I do. I want you."

"You have me," he said, and he made it sound as if there was so much more involved in those words than simply the physical.

But right now, I could only think of the physical side of things.

Touch.

Sensation.

Heat.

Allowing my thoughts to travel anywhere else would be too much. Too soon.

Too real.

He was right about that, whether I wanted to admit it or not.

"Show me what you want, then," Ethan said.

My pulse pounding in my ears, my breathing shaky

and shallow, I guided his hand to my breast. His large palm settled over me. He gently squeezed, and I closed my eyes with a soft sigh.

"More?" he asked.

I nodded.

He squeezed again, a bit harder this time, and my nipples hardened into tight balls.

I breathed in harshly against the sensation, allowing my head to fall back.

Ethan raised his other hand and covered my right breast with it, gently rolling his palm over my sensitive raised flesh.

"I want your mouth on me," I said.

"Over your clothes?"

I shook my head and reached for the hem of my top. He helped me lift it over my head, and I tossed it to the floor. His hands settled on my ribs, and he pressed his lips to the curve of my breast that was visible just over the top of my bra. My hands shook as I reached behind me and undid the clasp, but everything about Ethan was sure and steady.

He was a rock. My rock.

My eyes trained on his, I dropped the straps and let them fall from my arms.

Then he lowered his gaze and studied me—not just my bare breasts but the scar on my abdomen, the hint of my tattoo that was visible over the top of my pants, the minor dip in my waist, the slight bump of my lower belly, the one Hayes had hated, the one that had never flattened no matter how many crunches I'd done over the years—all the imperfections that made me *me*.

"You're so beautiful," Ethan said just before he crushed his mouth to my breast.

He swirled his tongue around my nipple and suckled my taut nub, all the while rolling my other nipple between his thumb and forefinger so gently I almost couldn't feel it. He kept one hand on my hip, holding me steady, keeping me grounded as my breathing turned ragged.

"More," I pleaded. "I need more."

"More how? What do you need more of?"

I needed more of *Ethan*, but I said, "Harder," because I couldn't quite figure out how to vocalize what I truly needed. The thought of putting it into words was enough to terrify me, and I didn't want there to be any fear involved in this. I wanted to lose myself in him. To forget all about everything that was wrong in my world, in my life, and only focus on the here and now.

He gave me what I asked for, lightly scraping one nipple with his teeth and rolling the other between his fingers with more pressure, and the insistent pressure building between my thighs turned to liquid heat.

A sharp crack of thunder split the silence that had been filled with only our breathing and moans, followed by a long, low rumble that seemed to go on forever. The entire house shuddered and reverberated from the intensity of the storm, which only added to the electricity pulsing between us. The lights flickered and then went out, but it didn't matter. We didn't need our eyes to see; our hands and tongues could see for us.

He shifted his attention to my other breast, and I collapsed back against the pillows, dragging him down with me.

"More," I pleaded, and I undid the button and fly of my jeans, dragging them down my hips before guiding his hand to my slick heat.

He gave me more, his mouth following the path of his hand. He licked and suckled, used his fingers and teeth and lips and tongue in ways I'd never experienced before, until I was rocking up my hips to meet him, my toes curling into the sheets as I cried out.

It was only when he wrapped me up in his arms a moment later, cradling me against his chest and whispering soothing words in my ear, that I realized I was actually crying. Hot tears dripped down my cheeks and landed on his chest.

"I'm sorry," he murmured. "I'm so sorry."

I shook my head. "No. Don't be sorry. I don't want you to be sorry."

"I shouldn't have done that. I shouldn't have gone so far."

"Ethan." I tipped his face up to meet mine, forcing him to look me in the eyes. "I wanted that," I insisted.

"But—"

"I *wanted* it," I repeated. "I want you."

And before he could come up with some other reason he shouldn't touch me, before he could devise an excuse to keep his hands off me any longer, I shifted off his lap and reached for his belt so I could undo the buckle, drawing the leather free from the loops.

"Natalie," he ground out when my fingers fumbled with his button and zipper, the hard evidence of his arousal pulsing against my fingertips.

I shot my eyes up to meet his gaze. "I want you," I repeated. "You told me you'd give me anything you can. I want you to give me this."

"You already have me," he said as I lowered his

pants and freed his length.

"I want all of you." Because I was almost positive he already had all of me.

Before he could come up with any more arguments, I dropped my mouth to place soft kisses over his crown, licking up the salty precum leaking from the tip.

"You don't have to do this," he said. "I don't expect you to—"

"I want this," I cut in, just before sliding the pointed tip of my tongue along the ridged underside of his penis.

He let out a ragged groan, and I felt the mattress shift beneath us as he inched back to brace himself against the headboard. When I took his crown between my lips and slowly lowered my mouth over him, taking almost all of his length, a soft hiss of breath flitted through his teeth.

I kept waiting for his hand to fall on the back of my head, guiding me to do what he wanted, pushing me to take more of his length, forcing me into gagging on him—but it never came. Ethan kept his hands fisted in the sheets beside his body, allowing me to set the pace.

I felt almost drunk on the power he was granting me over him.

His cock swelled in my mouth, and his balls tightened in my hand. I knew he was close, so I kept up my pace until he pulled away from me, saying, "You've got to stop, baby, I'm going to come." Then he hurried off the bed and stumbled to the bathroom, returning a few moments later with a warm, damp cloth that he passed into my hands.

Suddenly awkward and unsure of myself, I kept my

eyes down as I cleaned myself off.

Ethan sat on the edge of the bed beside me, his weight causing the mattress to dip. "I shouldn't have allowed that to happen," he said slowly.

"Why not? We both wanted it."

"What I want doesn't matter."

"It matters to me," I countered.

He sat there, the silence in the room heavy beneath the sounds of the thunderstorm raging outside.

I inched closer to him and reached for his hand. He allowed me to take it and twine our fingers together.

"I needed it," I said slowly. "I need more of it."

"I just don't want to push you into things I want when you aren't ready for them."

"You're not pushing me into anything, Ethan."

"I'm not so sure of that."

"Well, I am. Maybe that'll have to be good enough for the both of us."

"I want to give you what you need," he said. "I want to take care of you, but I can't put what I want first."

"Not even if it's what *you* need?" I said softly. "Don't you count in all of this? After everything your father put you through—"

"Not even if it's what I need," he said, cutting me off and speaking into the dark stillness between us.

"But what if what I need is you?"

He didn't have an answer for my question.

Chapter Twenty-Four

Ethan

The power had come back after about twenty minutes. By then, the storm had died down, so after I took a cold shower, I let Snoopy out of his Thundershirt. He followed me into my bedroom, and once I dragged on a pair of sweat pants and crawled into bed, he barked and jumped up to join me.

"You never sleep with me," I muttered, even as I shifted to the side so he could squeeze in. That dog always slept in Carter's room, even when Carter was with his mother.

I supposed all the storms we'd been experiencing lately were getting to him, though. He needed some companionship, and his boy wasn't here to give it to him.

I needed some companionship, too, but of an entirely different sort. I couldn't stop thinking about how good Natalie had felt beneath my hands, how soft her skin was, how passionately she'd responded to me. Not to mention the silky feel of her mouth on my cock. Fuck, but I'd never be able to forget how hard I'd come, how sweet she'd tasted, and how much I wanted to be inside her.

But that damned dog wouldn't get still. He kept nosing at the blankets and squirming to get closer to me, until he finally worked his way beneath the sheets and shifted all the way down to the foot of the bed to curl up around my feet. When I moved my toes because his wet nose was up against them, he barked and bit them.

"Pardon me for trying to get comfortable in my own fucking bed," I muttered. Not that I imagined I'd be very comfortable anytime soon. How could I be with the taste of Natalie still on my tongue and the memory of her silken skin imprinted on my brain?

He grumbled in response.

There wasn't much chance I'd be getting to sleep for hours. My mind was spinning too fast, too many things screaming for prominence in my brain: all the ways I'd fucked up by taking things too far with Natalie, all the ways my father could fuck up both her life and my own, how the hell I could protect her from Hayes, whether I'd landed myself in serious trouble with either the team or the league by spouting off in the press conference, what all of this would do to Carter, and possibly most importantly, how the hell I could ever give Natalie what she wanted without hurting her in the process.

I'd already allowed things to go too far. I should never have given in. But how could I tell her no when she asked me for what she wanted? The truth was, I didn't think I had the strength to deny her anything.

I lay in bed staring up at the ceiling for what felt like hours, but I couldn't sleep. I doubted I'd ever sleep again. Snoopy seemed just as restless as me, but maybe he was simply picking up on my own nervous energy and the electricity still in the air following the storm. But then a soft knock sounded at my bedroom door, and my heart turned over in my chest.

I froze, debating what to do.

"Ethan?" Natalie called out timidly. "Are you awake?"

Snoopy barked like a lunatic in response, jumping down to the floor and scurrying to the door, so whether I had intended to answer her or not, I couldn't feign sleep now.

I threw off the covers and glared at him on my way across the room to answer the door. In the dim light of my lamp, I could just make out the anxiety creasing Natalie's brows.

That felt like a punch to my gut. I wanted to kiss her tension away. But I was probably the cause of it. Or at least one of the causes.

I forced myself to keep my arms at my sides, my hands to myself.

"I couldn't sleep," she said after a pregnant pause.

I should never have touched her. I should have kept my fucking hands to myself. I'd probably hurt her leg, or maybe her lung, or lord only knew what else. "Are you in pain? We still have more of your meds some—"

"I can't sleep because I need to be with you," she cut in, and all the air whooshed out of my lungs in a single breath.

"You need…" I couldn't make myself finish the sentence because every nerve in my body was screaming to do things with her I had no business doing. More than we'd already done.

"I need to be with you," Natalie said, smooth and

calm. "I need you to hold me."

Well, hell. I couldn't very well deny her that. In fact, I didn't think I could deny her anything. I'd been trying to slow her down, but that wasn't going very well so far. I nodded curtly and backed up so she could slip past me.

Her hand trailed along my abdomen as she entered my bedroom, just a brush of her fingertips over my T-shirt, but it set every nerve ending in my body on edge. Especially when it combined with the sweet, delicate floral scent of her hair.

Just like that, I was hard enough to pound nails again. I closed my eyes, trying to get my dick under control.

But her scent was all around me. It wasn't just her hair. It was *her*. And now that I'd had a taste of her, I was like an addict—one taste would never be enough.

"You didn't put on your brace," I said.

She shook her head. "Didn't think I'd need it." She must have recognized my thoughts on the matter, because she pressed on before I could interrupt her. "I was careful—held on to the stair rail and everything."

"What if you need it in the morning?"

Natalie sat on the edge of my bed and shrugged. "Maybe Snoopy will go get it for me."

"More like I will."

She bit her lower lip, which drew my eye and made me think about how those lips tasted. Then she held out a hand for me, beckoning me closer.

I was powerless to stop my feet from closing the distance between us. When I took her hand, she drew me down onto the bed beside her, but she wouldn't meet my eyes, not even when I tried to tip her chin.

"Natalie…"

"Please," she whispered. "Let me stay with you. I need your arms around me. I need you to hold me."

My stomach in knots and my heart in tatters, I did the only thing I could: I pulled down the sheets, shoved Snoopy out of the way, and settled Natalie in my bed beside me. She rested her head on my shoulder so the sweet scent of her hair tickled my nostrils. Snoopy nosed his way under the covers again and curled up around my foot, and Natalie settled a hand over my stomach. Within minutes, they were both asleep.

But I lay awake for hours.

Because now, if Hayes's lawyers tried to come after me saying everything I'd claimed that asshole had done was all a lie and it was only because I'd wanted to get Natalie in my bed, there wasn't much I could say to dispute it. Maybe that wasn't what had been behind it initially—but here she was. In my bed. Curled up around me with a post-sex glow.

I might have just destroyed my own credibility.

If that fucker got off because I'd given in and taken things to another level with Natalie, I'd never be able to forgive myself.

Chapter Twenty-Five

Natalie

After everything I'd been through with Hayes, I never imagined I'd desire another man's touch, let alone trust any man enough to experience a sexual relationship again. But that was exactly what I wanted with Ethan—and I wanted far more than we'd done so far.

In my group therapy sessions, I had discovered that some of the women had completely lost all sexual desire due to the ways in which they'd been abused. Just the thought of experiencing something of that sort again took them straight back to the worst moments in their lives, and they fell into a downward spiral once again. They thought it was safer and better for their mental and emotional stability to be alone.

Others had seemingly gone the opposite direction, becoming addicted to sex, sometimes in almost perverse manners. Nothing they did was enough, and all of it left them feeling worse than ever before. There seemed no way for them to climb out of the pit, no way for them to move forward in a relationship that was built on trust and mutual respect, and certainly not love.

There didn't seem to be many who fell in the middle, and almost none of them had what could be considered a normal, healthy sex life. Maybe they *wanted* one, but they couldn't quite manage it. Only a small handful ever successfully got into monogamous relationships with decent partners, and fewer still maintained those relationships for very long.

I was determined to become one of the exceptions to the rule. I wasn't going to allow Hayes and his abuse to continue controlling me long after I'd gotten away.

I couldn't.

Besides, I had to remember that the other people in therapy with me were only recently removed from their situations.

The therapists always said that time was one of the most important factors in successfully moving on, right? And most of these men and women hadn't been free for much longer than I had. Maybe they just hadn't taken enough time before jumping back into the pool.

But had I?

I wasn't sure, but at the same time, I couldn't bear the thought of waiting any longer to build on what Ethan and I had started. I needed to prove to myself that I deserved a man in my life as good and strong and decent as Ethan.

He served as proof to me that someone could suffer incomprehensible abuse and still come out on the other side to live a good life. And there were more examples of the same everywhere I looked.

Dana Zellinger had been raped in college, but

she'd been happily married to her brother's best friend for something close to a decade now.

Viktoriya Chambers had been through countless forms of sexual abuse in her porn industry days, but she and Razor seemed to be getting along together just fine.

Everywhere I looked, I had strong women surrounding me who'd been through hell and back, and they were all the better for the crap they'd been put through. I had to believe that I could come out on the other side of this just as well as they had, because the opposite was too awful to contemplate.

And Ethan was *my* other side. He was my way out, both literally and figuratively.

I slept more soundly in his arms that night than I could remember doing, outside of my days in the hospital when I was so heavily drugged that all I could do was sleep. I slept the sleep of being at peace with my decisions and my future for the first time in far too long. For once, I actually *rested*.

When I awoke the next morning, though, it was to find Ethan staring at me, his forehead creased with all sorts of concerns that I didn't want to explore. I'd much rather remain in my afterglow bubble, pretending that real life couldn't intrude on this moment of perfect tranquility.

But Ethan wouldn't let me stay there. "If Hayes tries to say that we made it all up in order to justify your leaving him for me…"

"I don't want to think about Hayes right now," I complained, the afterglow fizzling down to nothing like a soda going flat.

"I don't want to, either. But we have to. Because you know he's thinking about us. About revenge.

About whatever the hell he thinks will get him off."

"There hasn't been anything else since your father coming down to talk to them, has there? Nothing new? Everything's quiet on that front."

"We can't fall for the trap of thinking no news is good news," Ethan said, and he pushed himself up to a sitting position in the bed. "Especially not—"

But he left that thought hanging.

"Especially not what?" I prodded.

"Especially not now that everything my father came down and told them might as well be true."

"You didn't hit Hayes because we had a relationship. We didn't have anything. Nothing. You didn't know me or anything about me. All you knew was what you saw. There wasn't anything more than that until now."

"But he's going to spin it that way. Or his lawyer will. You know they will."

I shook my head, forcing myself to sit up, as well. "Whatever's happening between the two of us has nothing to do with what Hayes did."

"The truth isn't going to hold much weight. There's no way we can prove it, anyway."

"But there has to be. Surely any jury with sense will have to see—"

"They'll see whatever the lawyers want them to see, Natalie. It's not supposed to be that way, but you know it is. That's how all of these cases work, especially when the defendant is famous. Almost every athlete in the last decade who's been accused of something like this has gotten away with it."

"So you're saying that I can't possibly win a case against him just because he's an athlete? Whether he's guilty or not?"

"I'm saying that the deck is stacked against us. How many guys like him can you think of who end up getting convicted of things like this? And even the guys who get convicted usually get off easy."

My eyes stung, but I refused to cry. I'd already shed more than enough tears over Hayes to last a lifetime. He didn't deserve any more of them.

Ethan reached for me, as if to draw me into an embrace, but I shifted away from him. If he wrapped me up in his arms now, I'd probably give in and cry, despite my best efforts.

"So do you want me to leave, then?" I asked meekly. "Is that what you're saying? You want me to find someone else to stay with?"

"I didn't say that. I don't want that." Ethan sounded defeated.

"Then what are you saying?"

"I'm saying maybe we shouldn't get involved like this. At least not right now. The timing is shit. That's all I'm saying."

"Is that what you want?" I shot my eyes up to meet his. They looked pained.

"No," he croaked, "it's not what I want. Not at all."

"Timing isn't everything. Sometimes the best things happen at the worst possible moment."

"And sometimes the worst things happen at the best moment."

"I don't think this could possibly fall into the *worst things* category," I said. "Not when we think about all of the other things we've been through. Both of us."

"It won't be very good if it ends with Hayes getting off."

"He might get off anyway," I pointed out.

"Not if I can help it."

"So is that more important to you?" I asked cautiously. "Making sure he pays for what he's done? That's more important than whatever we could have? Than what we might build together?"

For a long moment, Ethan wouldn't meet my eyes. He stared down at Snoopy and picked at a piece of lint on the bedding, anything to avoid looking at me. But when he finally looked up, he said, "I don't know. I honestly don't know, and that's what's killing me right now."

I nodded as if I understood, but I couldn't quite wrap my brain around it. Yes, Hayes had done awful things—to me—but I didn't want to give him the power to continue controlling me for the rest of my life. I wanted to take that power back, to reclaim it for myself. And in so many ways, it seemed that Ethan had done exactly that when it came to his father.

But not with this. In this one circumstance, it appeared that his father, and Hayes by extension, were still controlling Ethan's decisions, his life.

Maybe my hope of ever moving on in my life was all for naught.

Maybe I'd never be free, and what I saw in the other WAGs was nothing more than an illusion.

Maybe they weren't free, either.

Maybe Ethan was only putting on a show for the world, trying to pretend that he had moved on with his life, dealt with his demons, and was a well-adjusted, decent human being.

Maybe none of it was real. Maybe it was just a dream I was clinging to because I didn't have anything else to hold on to.

Cautious of my leg, I shifted until I could slip out

of the bed.

"Wait." He reached out a hand to stop me, but I shrugged him off and headed for the door. "Natalie, please," Ethan said.

"I need to go," I said, barely holding back a sob.

"Where?"

"I don't know." All I knew was I couldn't stay where I was any longer.

Chapter Twenty-Six

Ethan

Somehow, I'd convinced myself that Natalie would simply go back downstairs to her bedroom and stay there—that maybe she'd shut me out for a while, but then we could have a rational discussion and sort everything out like the adults we were.

It was easy to believe that when I heard the door to her room close, followed by a tense, crackling silence that ate away at me. The stillness allowed me to run through that conversation on repeat in my mind, listening to it again and again so many times that I couldn't help but think of all the ways I could have handled it better. Frankly, I doubted I could have handled it worse. Maybe if I'd *told* her to leave, but not much else would have qualified, and there wasn't a chance in hell I'd ever tell her anything of the sort.

The longer I lay there, the more certain I was that I'd fucked up royally. I couldn't let her leave. And not just because Hayes and his asshole friends and my father were all still out there, either. It was more than just a desire to protect her, to shield her from all the shittier parts of life that she'd already experienced more than her fair share of. Hell, it wasn't even just because I wanted to set an example for my kid of the kind of man I hoped he would grow up to become.

It went far deeper than all of that; I couldn't let her leave because I loved her. I needed Natalie in my life, and I needed her to know that. That explained my overprotectiveness of her, my need to be sure that Hayes paid for what he'd done to her. It explained the way my stomach clenched in fear anytime I thought of someone hurting her.

I loved her.

And sitting around and waiting for the right moment to tell her how I felt wouldn't do either of us any good.

Just when I'd finally made up my mind to go downstairs and admit to my own idiocy, Snoopy let out a bark and raced to the window the way he always did when a car pulled into the driveway.

Then the front door opened and closed.

No. This couldn't be happening.

When I reached the window, all I could see was an unfamiliar silver car driving away. I squinted to make out the license plate number, but it was no use—the car was already halfway down the street, too far away for me to see without superhuman bionic vision— and clearly, I was no superhero. I couldn't be any less heroic if I'd tried.

Fuck.

I bolted down the stairs and out the front door, but the car might as well have disappeared in thin air.

It was gone.

Natalie was gone.

I'd royally fucked up.

Snoopy yapped at my side, his ears low and his tail tucked between his legs. He knew something was wrong, too.

"Come on," I muttered, pointing him back into the house.

He barked at me, then followed it up with a low, discontented rumble.

"I know it," I said. "I was an idiot, okay? But what do you want me to do? I don't know where she went."

He barked again and then whined.

"Maybe she called one of the girls to come get her," I said, trying to explain it to myself as much as to the dog. I hoped that was the case. If she'd gone with Dana Zellinger or Tallie Fielding or one of the other WAGs, she'd be fine. Maybe not *emotionally* fine, but she'd be safe. And at the moment, safe would have to be good enough.

But I didn't recognize the car she'd gotten into—a fact that gnawed at me from the inside out.

I waited for Snoopy to do his business and then herded him back into the house. After starting a cup of coffee in the Keurig, I headed back upstairs and grabbed my phone off the charger. Then I shot off a quick text message to a few of the WAGs, asking if Natalie had contacted them and if she was on her way to their houses.

Within seconds, my phone started to light up with their responses.

London: *What the fuck did you do?*

Tallie: *She's not on her way here. At least*

not as far as I know.

Dana: *Why would she leave like that?*

London: *Because Bear did something stupid. Has to be.*

Dana: *I'm texting her now. Hold on.*

Viktoriya: *Not here.*

Ravyn: *Do you want us to help you look for her? Drew and I can be at your house in 10.*

London: *Dima says you're an idiot.*

London: *Actually, I'm not sure what he said. It was a mix of Russian, English, and Dima. But whatever it was, he's right, and I concur.*

London: *But seriously, what did you do?*

Dana: *She's not answering. I texted and called.*

Ravyn: *Should we file a missing person's report?*

Tallie: *She has to be missing for 24 hours first. Doesn't she?*

Dana: *I think so.*

Viktoriya: *Razor said the guys will all look for her.*

London: *She's not missing. She's here.*

And just like that, I could breathe again. I wasn't the praying sort, but for the first time in recent memory, I said a silent prayer of thanks. Maybe I'd been a huge idiot, but at least my idiocy hadn't resulted in Natalie falling into Hayes's hands again.

Me: *Tell her I'm on my way over to get her.*

London: *No, you're not. She doesn't want you to come.*

She didn't want me? *Ouch.* That hurt a lot more of me than merely my pride. But we needed to talk, and the only way that was going to happen was if I went over there and picked her up.

Me: *I'm coming anyway.*

London: *Dima will hold you down while I cut off your balls if you so much as step foot within fifty feet of my house. Understand? She doesn't want you here. Don't make me turn you into Reek. Or Varys. Or whoever.*

That hurt more than anything else could have. Not London's threats—but the fact that Natalie didn't want me to come get her. The fact that I'd fucked up so badly that she'd run from me.

I was supposed to be protecting her from all the

shit in the world, but instead, I was causing even more of it.

I wanted to hit something. Someone.

No, not just any random *someone*. I wanted to hit Hayes. And my father. And everyone else who had played any part in hurting Natalie.

But by that standard, I ought to hit myself.

I threw a pillow at the wall, more disappointed in myself than I could ever remember feeling before. Snoopy whimpered and jumped up to sit beside me, burrowing his face in my lap for comfort.

Not that it helped.

Nothing could help me now.

Chapter Twenty-Seven

Natalie

I couldn't cry.

I wanted to, actually. I'd been trying, hoping it would help. Breaking down for a bit might make it feel a lot better. Sometimes, nothing would help other than having a good blubber-fest and getting all the hurt and anger and disappointment out of your system, and right now seemed as though it should be one of those times.

But no tears would come.

My eyes remained dry, scratchy...raw, almost to the point of pain, but not quite. At this juncture, even pain would be welcome, because it would mean I felt something. Anything.

Instead, I felt numb.

I didn't want to be numb. I wanted to experience it all right now, so I could get it over with and move on. Putting it off wouldn't help anything. Through all the years I'd spent with Hayes, I'd learned that delaying the inevitable only made it worse when it finally happened—whatever *it* might be. Better to face whatever crap life would throw at me head on, rather than trying to hide from the unavoidable.

Knowing all of that didn't help, though. Despite my best efforts, I couldn't make the tears fall. It was as if everything inside me had gone dry and hollow, leaving me nothing but an echoing chamber of emptiness.

"I'll rip his head off next time I see him," London practically spat. "What the hell was he thinking, letting you run off like that?"

London's fury only made the emptiness inside me build. Because, whether I should be or not, I wasn't mad. I couldn't drum up any anger inside to fill the void. Instead, all I had was a horrifically dull ache that gnawed away at my stomach.

"He didn't know I was leaving," I said. "I didn't tell him."

"Don't get me started on how stupid *you* were," she shot over her shoulder at me from the low kitchen island, where she was chopping up a cucumber with a ferocity that should have had me quaking where I stood. "Because that asshole and his friends are out there, and while you were all alone, they could have done anything to you and you wouldn't have had any way of letting us know you were in trouble. But right now, my mad is all directed at that overgrown idiot who let you walk out by yourself. You don't want me to turn it around on you."

Her son crawled over near her wheelchair and tried to climb up the spokes of her wheel, but Dima swooped in from around the corner. He lifted the boy out of harm's way, giving me a wink before whisking the toddler into another room.

"It's not like I just walked out and wandered around aimlessly, waiting for Hayes to come and attack me."

"No, but you didn't tell anyone where you were going, either. What if we weren't at home?"

"Then I would have gone to Ravyn's house."

"Try a call first next time," London said, glowering. "Or even a text. *Something.* You had an awful lot of people worried about you." She reached for a tomato and started attacking it just as fervently as she'd gone at the cucumber. The cutting board was beginning to look like a crime scene.

Her admonishment stung, almost as much as Ethan's easy dismissal of me. Maybe he hadn't told me to leave, but he might as well have. Telling me that getting revenge against Hayes at some point in the future was more important than helping me get what I needed in the present was like a knife in my gut.

Mainly because it proved my fears were valid.

Maybe Ethan seemed whole and complete on the surface. Maybe it appeared he had gotten his life together after all the horrors his father had put him through.

But in the end, he was just as messed up as the rest of us.

He didn't have it all figured out. He hadn't moved on. All he'd done was build a wall around himself, using that protective barrier to hide the ugliest parts of himself. And maybe he was able to keep that ugliness at bay most of the time—but it would always rear up again at the worst possible moment.

If I spent more time around Dana Zellinger and Viktoriya Chambers and all of the other WAGs who'd been through traumatic events in their past, I knew I'd find the same. They might appear to be coping well on the surface, but peeling back a layer at a time was bound to produce an unsightly, battered core, just like mine.

So I was right—I'd never be free of Hayes. And my core might just be the foulest, most abused of them all. I would never be whole again, and I couldn't allow myself to believe otherwise. I'd only be setting myself up for a greater disappointment than I'd ever known. Expecting the worst was the only safe way for me to go through life from here on out.

But London was still glaring at me and wielding a butcher's knife.

"Sorry," I mumbled. I reached for a carrot and a vegetable peeler so I could help her out and so I'd have something to do with my hands. "I didn't mean for anyone to worry about me." For that matter, I hadn't realized how many people really *would* worry about me. Hayes had kept me in his bubble for so long that I hadn't had friends in the outside world for close to a decade. I still wasn't used to it.

And maybe I shouldn't *get* used to it, either. Because then I'd only be setting myself up for more disappointments in the future.

"Well, what the hell did you think we'd do?" London shot back. "People care about you, you know. A lot of people. You're not alone, even if you feel like you are sometimes. And it isn't just us. Bear's going nuts."

"Good," I said before I could think better of it.

London stopped chopping long enough to raise her brow in question.

I shrugged. "Maybe he needs to go nuts for a

while. Maybe it'll help him realize what's more important."

"So what's more important?"

I stopped myself from saying, "Me," just in the nick of time. Believing I was important—to Ethan or anyone else—would only serve to set myself up for more heartache. Instead, I shrugged.

London's glare could melt stone. "That's not going to cut it with me, missy. What's more important than making sure you're safe?"

"There's no such thing as safe. No one can promise me that."

She scowled. "Someone's been watching too much *Game of Thrones*. You're not Sansa Stark. And she's done a pretty damned good job of making sure she stays safe, now that she's old enough and wise enough to figure out who to trust, anyway. And you're plenty old enough and wise enough to see that, too."

"This is real life," I said. "We're not in some TV show. Things don't work out for the best in the real world."

"Sometimes they do," London countered.

I chose not to argue with her over that. Arguing was exhausting, and it seemed to be London's favorite pastime.

"So what, then?" she demanded. "Make sure that asshole and his friends can't hurt you anymore?"

"No one can make sure of that!" I said. "That's not possible. He'll always be able to hurt me."

"Sure he can. If you let him...and you practically sent him an open invitation. Flashing neon lights. Dancing bears in pink tutus. Fireworks and a concert band blaring out into the night. Welcome mat under his feet. All that jazz."

"I'm not talking about that. Physical pain is nothing. Not compared to this. I'm talking about inside." With those words, suddenly all the tears that wouldn't come earlier started forcing their way to the forefront.

London scowled. Something told me she wasn't comfortable with tears. "So am I, dummy," she said.

I laughed despite myself. She was right. I was a dummy.

She set down her knife and veggies, then wheeled around to the other side of the kitchen island, and before I knew what was happening, she'd pulled me in for a hug and I was blubbering on her shoulder.

I cried so hard for so long that I almost didn't notice it when strong arms came around me from behind and lifted me away from London.

Ethan's arms.

And even though I'd thought I wanted him to stay away, I found myself curling in toward the safety and comfort he presented. Façade or not, it was a nice fantasy to escape into, if only for a little while.

"I thought I told you she didn't want you," London grumbled threateningly.

"I'm not scared of Dima," he replied.

"It's me you should be scared of, not Dima."

But Ethan didn't pay her any attention, instead carrying me into the living room and drawing me onto his lap on the couch.

Despite my better intentions, I melted against him. His heat was intoxicating. His strength was a comfort. His nearness was everything.

"You scared the shit out of me," he said after a long silence.

I tried to shrug him off, because I wasn't

particularly in the mood to hear about his fears. He could have prevented his own fears from becoming an issue if he would just forget about his desire for Hayes's comeuppance. But Ethan didn't seem to be in the mood to let me push his fears aside.

He tipped my chin up until I finally met his eyes. "I know I screwed up. I know we need to talk about this—all of it—but we can't do that if you run off."

"You also can't do it if you act like an overbearing, authoritarian moron," London called out from the kitchen.

"Trying to rectify that," Ethan grumbled.

"Try harder," she shot back. "You need to grovel."

"Grovel?"

"Grovel. Beg. Plead. Admit you're an idiot and you're going to try not to be an idiot anymore, but you're probably going to do some more stupid things again at some point in the future, so you're begging for her forgiveness. For this time. And for the next time. And for all the times after that. If you're anything like my husband, you're going to have to get really good at this whole groveling thing, so you might as well start now."

But that wasn't what I wanted. Maybe I didn't know exactly what I wanted, but it wasn't this. "You don't have to—"

"I was an idiot," he said, cutting me off, and I was so stunned that I couldn't stop him.

London wheeled around the corner, a kitchen towel draped over her lap with the butcher knife resting on top of it. "An overbearing one. You thought you knew best, and you tried to make Natalie go along with what you wanted, whether *Natalie* thought it was best for her or not."

But Ethan didn't even bother looking over at her. His attention was solely on me. "I didn't listen. I thought I knew what was best for everyone—both of us—and I made a decision and expected you to go along with it, whether it was best for you or not. That's one of my biggest issues—you can ask Carter's mom. It's one of the reasons we couldn't make things work out. But I'm trying, Nat. And I need you to try, too. When I'm an idiot, I need you to stand your ground and tell me I'm being an idiot instead of running away. It's the only way I'll learn. And it's the only way we can make this work."

"And it's the only way we can all be sure that asshat and his dipshit buddies aren't going to do something to you that we can't undo," London interjected.

I was about to tell her off and ask her to leave so Ethan and I could have a private conversation, but Ethan beat me to it.

"Would you give us some privacy so I can explain to Natalie that the biggest reason I'm an idiot when it comes to her is because I love her?"

It seemed as if the entire world switched to slow motion at that moment. Dima came in and lifted London out of her chair, tossing her over his shoulder in a fireman carry and carrying her out of the room despite her vocal protests. Erik followed them, cackling with glee at the sight of his mother pounding on his father's shoulders while cursing up a storm. Ethan dragged a hand over his face, and a pained sound seemed to come from his chest.

But I couldn't process any of it. "You love me?" I murmured.

"I love you," he croaked. "And the last thing in the

world I would ever want to do is hurt you in any way. But apparently I can't even try to protect you from all the shit going on in our world without hurting you in the process. And then putting you in more danger, too."

"You didn't put me in danger."

"Might as well have. I ran you off. I didn't stop you from going."

"But that was my choice. It was my turn to be stupid."

"How about we both stop being stupid for a while? Can we make a pact about that?"

My stomach clenched. "If I come home with you again, I need to be with you. To truly be with you, no matter what it means for the case or how Hayes and his lawyers might try to spin things. Can you give me that? Because if you can't, if that isn't going to work for you, I need to figure out where else I can go. I'll have to start figuring out how to move on with my life without you."

He stared down at our joined hands in my lap for a long time—so long I feared he would tell me no.

"I don't think I'm strong enough to let you go," he finally said. "Whatever you want, whatever you need from me, it's yours." He kissed my cheek, and his lips came away wet from my tears. "I'm yours."

"I'm yours, too."

"So does this mean I don't get to cut off his balls?" London called out impatiently from the other room. "I really, really want to cut off his balls. My knife is ready. I've been itching to try it out on someone."

"Crazy woman," Dima grumbled. "Why you're obsessed with his balls?"

"You don't want me to cut off your balls, instead,

do you? Because I will."

"Good thing you can't walk," he replied, and he came back into the living room without her, plopping down into her wheelchair and rolling his eyes dramatically. Erik followed him and climbed onto his lap.

"I can still get around without my chair, you know," London shouted from the kitchen. "Might take me longer, but I'm coming for you."

Ethan and I both laughed. It felt good to laugh.

Chapter Twenty-Eight

Ethan

I loved Natalie.

That was something I couldn't lie about, not even if she'd be better off not knowing. If she didn't know, then she couldn't accidentally say something to a police officer or a lawyer, she couldn't accidentally bring it up in court if it came to that. But I couldn't keep it to myself any longer, and so now it was out there.

With any luck, it wouldn't come back to bite us both in the ass.

We were back at my place after I finally convinced London that I wasn't anywhere close to finished with all the groveling I needed to do.

And now I needed to set about showing Natalie how much I loved her. This time, I couldn't hold back. Words weren't enough. Especially not since some of my actions proved my words to be true while others made me out to be a liar.

Maybe it was the middle of the day, but I didn't care. As soon as we were back in my house, I took

Natalie straight to my bed and kicked Snoopy out of the room, ignoring his whine of protest.

She was already reaching for me before I made it back to the bed, using her other hand to fumble with the latches on her brace.

"Let me," I said, because it would be quicker. I unhooked all the clasps as fast as I could and carefully took it off her leg.

But there was nothing careful about the way Natalie was reaching for me. She had one hand digging into my hair and the other making a fist in my shirt, tugging me until I almost toppled onto her.

And then everything was a blur of need. Clothes flying everywhere. Tongues and teeth and hands on every bit of bare flesh we could find. Skin, sweat, salt... My mind went blank to anything other than the woman beneath me. She tasted like heaven.

With surprisingly strong and determined hands, she pulled me closer.

"Slow down, baby," I said, dusting her collarbone with my lips.

"I can't. I can't slow down. I need you."

But she already had me, in more ways than she could possibly understand. I'd meant it when I told her I was hers. She owned me in every way that mattered.

I slid a hand between our bodies. Slick heat welcomed my touch. She felt so good I couldn't stop my groan as I pumped my fingers into her core a few times, imagining how that same heat would feel around my dick.

"Please," she said, her voice soft and shaking as she dug her fingers into my shoulders.

I rolled the pad of my thumb over her clit,

spreading her wetness and making her writhe beneath me.

"I want you inside me," Natalie ground out, her entire body shaking with the need for release. She bit her lower lip and tried to glare at me, but she was too close to orgasm for that to really work out.

"Not yet."

She whimpered in frustration.

"I want to watch you come first," I explained.

Then I put all my focus on her—watching the way her eyes shifted focus when I altered the way I teased her clit, listening for the slight change in her breathing when I picked up the pace, noticing the gradual shift as her skin turned from pale pink to a dusky rose.

Her orgasm was so quiet I would have missed it if not for the way her mouth fell open and her eyes scrunched closed.

"You're so fucking perfect," I said as I lowered my head for a kiss. She tasted like apples and rain. I wanted to drown in her, and she seemed willing to open up and let me do exactly that.

Shifting my weight off of her, I reached for a condom in my nightstand and shucked it free from the wrapper. I'd barely rolled it on before Natalie was trying to drag me back on top of her.

She shifted her hips and raised her knees, her body becoming a welcoming cocoon. I sank to my knees and buried myself in her in a single stroke.

Her heat was so intense I almost melted. It'd been too long for me—much too long since I'd experienced the pleasure of a woman's body, and even longer since I'd been with a woman I loved. I tried to hold my weight off her—the thought of hurting her was more than I could bear—but she wrapped her arms and legs around me, clinging to me, and it was all I could do not to lose control.

It was all happening too fast. I wanted to last, but every time I tried to slow down, she angled her hips in a new way or slid her hands across my ass, grabbing hold of my flesh and dragging me back to her.

"You're holding back," she said, panting. "Don't do that. I need you."

"I'm not. And I already told you—you have me."

She took my face between both of her hands, forcing me to look deep into her eyes. "You're holding back," she repeated.

"I don't want to hurt you."

Natalie kissed me hard, her tongue working against mine the way she'd used it on my cock before. Her teeth nipped my lip—just hard enough to make me suck in a breath of air—before she released me. "You won't hurt me," she said adamantly. "That's not who you are."

She had a lot more faith in me than I did where that was concerned. I'd already hurt her enough that she'd felt the need to leave.

But Natalie seemed uninclined to give an inch on this. She fisted a hand in my hair, kissing me with tongue and teeth and fervent hunger. Wrapping her legs around my waist and fusing our bodies together with a power in her thighs I didn't know she possessed, she drew me deeper than ever.

After a few more blind thrusts, her pussy clenched and quivered around me, which was all it took to send me over the edge. I buried my face in a pillow next to her head and shouted with my release.

When I rolled off her, I drew her over with me

until she was halfway draped across my body. Her limbs were warm and lax. Warm breath feathered across the slick skin of my chest.

She tipped her face up toward mine and stared into my eyes, her fingertips dancing gently over my chest.

"If you keep touching me like that, I'll be ready for round two in about twenty seconds," I said, trying to laugh it off even though I was entirely serious.

A soft chuckle fell through her lips, followed by her tongue darting out to wet them again. "Ethan?" she said, suddenly tentative and uncertain, when moments before she'd been demanding and in control.

My gut clenched at the return of her timidity. "Hmm?" I replied, hoping I hadn't gone and fucked up again already.

"I think I love you, too," she said.

Her eyes fluttered closed, and within moments, her breathing evened out. She was asleep before I could question her. *She thinks she loves me?* Did that mean she wasn't sure, or did she not know how to be certain? Or maybe she was just scared to admit the truth.

Whatever it was, I wouldn't be getting any sleep for a long time to come. My chest felt full and heavy, like my heart was too big to fit and my lungs were over capacity.

Natalie loved me. Maybe she wasn't sure about it yet, but I was. She was choosing to trust me with her heart—her broken, battered, bruised heart.

The weight of responsibility that came with her love was easily as heavy as what I felt when it came to raising Carter.

I couldn't fuck this up.

Chapter Twenty-Nine

Natalie

"Good news," Detective Andrews said over the phone about a week later.

Ethan and I had been getting along better than ever, both of us doing everything in our power to make this work. He wasn't making decisions for me anymore, and I was talking to him openly and honestly whenever anything came up. So far, so good.

But our fledgling relationship wasn't the only thing on our minds. In fact, there were much more pressing matters weighing on us—namely Hayes and his friends, and what was happening in the case.

Of late, there hadn't been much, and that had us both on edge.

"Good news?" I pressed the button to put him on speakerphone so Ethan could hear everything the detective had to say, too.

Ethan raised a brow in question, but he kept quiet.

"The prosecutors have offered Barnes and Lipscomb a deal if they cooperate, and they've agreed to it."

I still wasn't used to anyone referring to Alex and Jason by their surnames, even if I knew exactly who Detective Andrews meant. It took me a moment to shake my brain into action so I could catch up. "Okay," I murmured.

But Ethan wouldn't be so easily satisfied. "How the hell is letting those scumbags off easy good news?" he demanded.

"They won't be getting off easy," the detective insisted. "Just a lighter sentence in exchange for helping us nail Lennon for his part in all of this. They'll still serve time, but we'll be able to charge him finally—and we can make sure we get him on the more serious charges this way."

"But how…?" My question trailed off, because I couldn't even put all my warring thoughts into words.

Mainly because Ethan looked livid.

"Barnes and Lipscomb have agreed to tell a grand jury that they were acting on Lennon's orders. They'll get a lighter sentence, but they'll still do time. We'll get Lennon to show up in court under some pretense or another—we can tell him that they're going to testify to their guilt, and he'll want to be there to make certain they don't rat him out for his part in things—and when he walks in, they can arrest him under a sealed indictment warrant."

"A sealed warrant?" I repeated.

"They do this all the time when it's someone well known. Actors, musicians, athletes, politicians… It's a way to be sure he shows up and doesn't skip out of town."

"Does Natalie have to be there?" Ethan asked. "I don't want her anywhere near that—"

"She doesn't have to be present," he cut in before

Ethan could really begin to rant about Hayes. "And at that time, we can get the judge to issue a criminal court protective order against all three of them, too. It'll give Natalie a higher degree of protection than what she's already got. Police officers are more likely to treat it seriously."

"So she doesn't have to testify," Ethan said.

"Not yet. Whenever the case gets to trial, that'll be a different matter."

"But I have time to get ready for that," I put in.

"And the prosecution will have some people who'll help you prepare, too. You won't go into the situation blindly."

I wasn't sure I'd ever be ready, no matter how well they tried to prepare me for it. How could I walk into a court, with Hayes sitting across from me, leering at me, trying to stare me down, and tell the world all the things he'd done to me? Just the thought of it made my skin crawl.

"You've got time to prepare for that," the detective agreed.

He went over a few more details with us. The plan was for this to take place on Tuesday—just after Carter's next weekend visit with Ethan.

That little boy would be a welcome distraction. And a good reason for the two of us to put the brakes on how fast things had been moving between us. Time for me to move back down to my room and stop sleeping in Ethan's bed for a while.

Kicking Snoopy out of the bedroom and closing the door was one thing; having Carter attempting to sleep in the next room would be something else entirely. I didn't know how Ethan felt about introducing the idea of our relationship to his son, but

I knew I wasn't ready for him to find me naked in his father's bed or anything of that sort. I wasn't sure I'd ever be ready for that.

"Thanks again for keeping us updated," Ethan said after the detective answered about a dozen more of his questions while my mind drifted, and then we hung up.

"See? It's going to be all right. Everything's going to work out," I said, admittedly trying to convince myself as much as I wanted to convince him. Snoopy shoved his head onto my lap, so I scratched his ears distractedly.

Ethan's look said he didn't want to concede the point, but he was choosing not to argue with me. "Let's not get too excited until the guy's behind bars with his buddies, all right? Because I don't know how well I can breathe until then."

"You'd better figure out how to breathe before Carter's flight lands. He'll run you ragged."

Snoopy's ears perked up at the mention of Carter's name, but he didn't lift his head off my lap, even though his eyes were moving back and forth between me and Ethan.

"Yes, your boy's coming home soon," Ethan said, scratching the dog's back.

Snoopy barked and wagged his tail.

"It's amazing how much he understands," I said.

"Carter's a smart kid."

I laughed. "I meant Snoopy. But yeah, Carter, too." Which was exactly the lead-in I needed to guide our conversation.

"You have no idea. I swear, this dog always knows everything that's going on, sometimes before I do. I'm surprised he didn't manage to stop you from leaving…"

"He's not as attached to me as he is to you and Carter."

"That's changing," Ethan said. "He's getting to be as attached to you as I am. Look whose lap he's got his head on."

"That's just because I'm rubbing his ears."

"Yeah, if he could talk, he'd tell you to stop doing that in about a decade, but no sooner."

"I don't know. Once Carter gets here, Snoopy'll probably want to go chase him around for a while."

"And when they're both exhausted, they'll come back to your lap for ear rubs and story time or something."

This wasn't the smoothest segue ever, but I knew I had to get there eventually. "Speaking of Carter," I said a lot more hesitantly than I'd intended.

Ethan met my eyes. "I've already told him."

"You've already…?"

"Told him that we're together. And that I love you."

"You've already told your son that you love me?" I hadn't been expecting to cry. To be honest, I wasn't sure what I'd expected. But there were hot tears trying to spring free, and I had to blink them back.

"I did. And I talked to Kinsey about it, too."

"You talked to your ex about me?"

"She's Carter's mother. She needs to know who's in my life, because it means you're in Carter's life, too. We may not be married anymore, but we're still a team when it comes to our son. So she needs to know when I want someone else to be part of the team." He stopped scratching Snoopy and reached for my hand, threading our fingers together right around the same time as my heart stopped beating and lodged itself somewhere in the vicinity of my throat, preventing my stomach from emptying its contents. "She wants to come down at Thanksgiving to meet you," Ethan continued. "The team's at home then, so this year I'm supposed to have Carter for Thanksgiving anyway, and she'll get him at Christmas. But she thought that would be a good time for her make a trip down. We can all have Thanksgiving together as a family. Is that okay? Kinsey coming to meet you?"

"She wants to meet me?" I spluttered, because I couldn't wrap my head around it.

"I know it's a lot to take in—"

"It's not that," I cut in. "I just— I don't—" I took a breath, trying to slow my thoughts so I could get a grasp on them before I said something stupid. "It's just—do you think we're jumping in too fast?"

"You were the one who said you needed to really be with me or you couldn't stay."

"I know. And I meant it. I'm just…"

Scared.

That was the word that refused to come out. It was right on the tip of my tongue, but I couldn't set it free.

Ethan stroked the back of my hand, the same way he'd been stroking Snoopy's back. Soothing. Calming. "Am I moving things too fast for you? I shouldn't have told you I loved you so soon. I should've—"

"No," I cut in.

"No?" His hand stopped moving, the pad of his thumb just tickling the side of my pinky finger.

"I'm glad you told me," I forced out, silently cursing myself over the way I was bungling this. "It's too easy for me to think that no one loves me, even when so many people do everything in their power to *show* me they do."

"So many people," he murmured, sounding hurt.

"I know you love me," I said. "You'd have to, or you never would have done so much for me. You never would have—" But I was too choked up to continue.

"But you don't love me? Is that it?"

He sounded so calm. How could he be calm when everything inside me was like a tornado? My thoughts were whirling out of control, and my emotions wouldn't settle.

"I feel like I'm taking advantage of you," I said, and I immediately wished I could take the words back, because they weren't even remotely enough to convey everything I was feeling. But I couldn't make any more words come out, or else I'd fall apart.

"You're not taking advantage of me," Ethan said.

"It's not just you. It's everyone! London and Dana and Tallie and Ravyn—"

"They've all been helping you out because they care about you. You're not taking advantage of anyone. You needed help, and they care, so they helped."

"But with you…"

"I love you," he repeated. "That's all that matters to me. You don't have to tell me you love me. You don't have to love me. If I get hurt because you can't love me in return, that's all on me, but it's not going to stop me from loving you. It's too late for that. It's been too late for that for a long time."

"But what if I—"

Ethan reached up with his big hand and used the

pad of his thumb to brush the tears from my cheeks. "What if you what?" he prompted.

"What if I can't love you back the way you love me? What if I'm too scared to give someone that kind of power over me?"

For a long time, he stared down at Snoopy, scratching the dog's belly and ears. But then he looked up again and met my eyes, and he said, "Then my heart will hurt for you, because no one stepped in and got you out in time. It would mean that no one helped before the scars were too deep. That I didn't get there soon enough."

That only made me cry harder. "But what about you?"

"What about me?" he asked softly.

I shrugged because I couldn't find the words.

"You've already made a mark on me, Nat. You're already part of me—as deep as anything. So if I have to let you go…yeah. It'll gut me. But I can handle my pain a hell of a lot better than I can handle being responsible for causing you any more heartache than you've already lived through. I'm not strong enough for that."

If he wasn't strong enough, there wasn't a chance in hell I was.

Chapter Thirty

Ethan

"Mrs. K said we have to read a whole book every day this weekend. I have to give a book report on them when we go back on Tuesday." Carter had his Tow Mater backpack perched high on his shoulders while I carried his Lightning McQueen suitcase and Natalie walked alongside us.

"Three books, since Monday's a holiday?" I asked.

"What holiday?"

"It's not really a holiday, I don't think. It's just a teacher in-service day."

"Is that jail for teachers or something?"

I laughed. "You'd have to ask Mrs. Kuchner."

"I think it's jail."

"Whether it's jail or not, you've got the day off."

"Right. She said we can take Monday off. Just two books."

"You sure about that?" I asked. Something told me he might be either remembering incorrectly or telling me a fib to get out of doing the work. But it wasn't really in his nature to not be truthful, so I knew I should give him the benefit of the doubt. His days of making up lies were sure to come somewhere down the line, but I hoped I had almost another decade before I had to worry about that.

Carter jumped over a painted line in the parking lot, picking up his usual game. "Positive. Just two books this weekend."

"Still, that's a lot of reading," I said, biting back a grin. "How are you going to have time for all that when we have hockey games to go to?"

He turned around and grinned at me and Natalie. "Back-to-back, right? Two home games this weekend." He turned around, skipped across another line, and stood on one foot for as long as he could maintain his balance, then made another big leap to get to a clearing.

"That's right. One tomorrow night and another on Sunday afternoon."

"I can bring my book to the games and read at inna-mission."

"You won't be watching all the fun?" Natalie caught my eye, barely containing her laughter over the way he'd mispronounced the word.

I winked at her.

"Nah. That stuff's boring. I'd rather watch the hockey."

I noticed that she didn't try to correct him, though. One more way she was a perfect fit in our lives. I just hoped I could convince her to agree—and to accept and admit that she loved me.

She did. I knew it. She was just scared, which was understandable, given her history. Eventually, she'd come to accept that opening herself up to love was the only way to get through life, even though she'd been through hell and back.

I already knew how Carter and Snoopy felt about the matter without even asking them. They were both open books. If you showed them kindness, they loved you in return. Simple. Which meant they loved Natalie.

And Kinsey approved, even though she hadn't met Natalie yet. My ex didn't need to meet her to approve of my choice. Carter's mom had always wanted the best for me, and as long as I was happy, she was happy, too. She knew I wouldn't invite a woman into my life—and Carter's life, by extension—if it wasn't someone who belonged with us.

I trusted her in the same way. She hadn't dated anyone in a while, but I hoped that would change soon. She deserved to have love in her life again, and it could only be a good thing for Carter to have more role models to look up to.

Three or four parents had to be better than two, right? Something like that.

He wobbled and almost fell over, but he reached up and grabbed hold of Natalie's hand to steady himself. She was still wearing the boot these days, but she never even used the crutches for balance anymore. It wouldn't be much longer before she was back to whatever her new normal would be.

And I intended for me, Carter, and Snoopy to be a big part of that new normal.

"And we can read together before bed, too," I added.

"No! I have to read it myself." He was offended almost to the point of being scandalized. I loved that he wouldn't take the easy path and was determined to do things for himself. It would serve him well for years to come.

"Well, you can read it to me. Bedtime reading doesn't have to be me reading to you," I pointed out.

"Maybe Natalie can come read with me and Snoopy."

I chortled at his less-than-subtle hint. My kid knew what he wanted. "Maybe she can," I said.

"She can," Natalie put in. "What books are you reading?"

"I've got *The Adventures of Taxi Dog* and *Dogku*."

She glanced at me with a question in her eyes, and I shrugged. I hadn't ever heard of them, but that didn't mean much.

"They sound fun," she said.

"I thought Snoopy would like them because they're about dogs. I got 'em at the libary."

"It's always important to think about what books your puppy will enjoy most," I said, trying to keep a straight face.

"Don't make fun, Dad. Snoopy likes to read with me."

"Snoopy likes to do anything with you. Because you're you. He's your dog, and you're his kid, and that's what dogs do. They like hanging out with their kids."

"I think Snoopy's pretty smart that way," Natalie said.

"He knows he's got a good deal with you, bud," I added. "He lucked out, getting the best kid in the world to have as his boy."

"He's a really smart dog," Carter added matter-of-factly. "I'm gonna teach him how to read."

Natalie chuckled. "Sounds like quite a task. I've never heard of a dog that can read."

"Snoopy will learn. He can already find which cup has a ball under it. He's magic."

"He can?"

"Yup!"

Because he watches Carter hide the ball, I mouthed to Natalie over Carter's head as I fished my keys out of my pocket and clicked the button to open my trunk.

She had the good grace not to laugh out loud, but her amusement was fully evident in her eyes.

"Everything in the back," I said, loading Carter's suitcase inside before reaching for his backpack.

"Can I keep my iPad to play in the car?"

I narrowed my eyes in mock scorn. "Depends. What are you playing?"

"Angry Birds Blast! And I'm stuck on level seventy-nine."

"That's a tough one," I said, not that I had any idea what level seventy-nine was. I'd never played the game before. "Better work hard on it in the car."

He climbed into the back and buckled himself into his booster seat while Natalie and I both got in the front. "Are we getting Braum's for dinner?" Carter asked.

The last time I'd promised him Braum's was the day I'd pulled Natalie out of that house. Our ice cream date hadn't quite panned out, and there weren't any Braum's locations in Michigan. His only opportunity to pig out on their burgers, crinkle-cut fries, and ice cream was when he came to visit me.

"You okay with burgers tonight?" I asked Natalie as I pulled out into traffic. "They've got some healthier things, too. Salads and chicken sandwiches and whatnot."

"And ice cream!" Carter said.

CATHERINE GAYLE

"I'm always down for ice cream."

"Then it's a date," I said.

She didn't attempt to correct me or deflect the idea of us going on a date. And it didn't matter to me that Carter would be with us—in my mind, it *was* a date. A family date.

I could get used to this idea.

No, that wasn't exactly true. I was already used to it, and I wanted it to become our permanent reality.

Carter, Snoopy, and I needed Natalie in our lives every bit as much as she needed us.

Chapter Thirty-One

Natalie

Carter made me laugh so hard my ribs hurt. But this was a much better sort of ache than what I'd felt before. There was just something infectious about that little boy—the way he swirled ketchup and mustard together to make a dip for his fries, the giggle when he flipped his spoon and it sent ice cream smothered in strawberry sauce and hot fudge flying into his father's hair, the care he took in wiping his sticky hands clean before reaching for my hand when we were leaving. And then there was the way he got upset when we were leaving and he realized he'd forgotten to buy a treat for Snoopy.

"He needs a sundae," Carter insisted, stopping in his tracks when we were halfway across the parking lot. "Hot fudge and strawberry like mine."

Ethan appeared to be having great difficulty not laughing. "Dogs can't have chocolate. No fudge. How about we just get him a cup of vanilla froyo? I bet he'll think that's the best thing ever. And we can get a lid on it so it won't melt or spill in the car."

After a couple of minutes haggling in the parking lot, it was agreed that Snoopy would get vanilla frozen yogurt in a cup, but Carter insisted on a taking a waffle cone with us, as well, so his puppy wouldn't think he was missing out.

When we got back to Ethan's house, Carter raced inside without bothering to bring his backpack or even his iPad. All he bothered with was the treat, leaving the rest for his father to deal with.

I walked through the garage door to the sound of happy barking and a giggling boy. Snoopy and Carter had met up in a tackle-hug in the middle of the kitchen floor, and Snoopy had the boy pinned beneath him while he licked the child's face.

"Snoopy, stop! You're going to spill your ice cream!" Carter squealed, but the dog didn't seem to care. He was too excited about his boy being home to worry about trivial things like making a mess in the kitchen.

Ethan carried all of Carter's things past him and up the stairs.

I sidestepped the pile of fun, careful not to step on fingers, tails, or toes, and headed for the living room.

When Ethan came back down the stairs, he had his cell phone pressed to his ear. "You're sure?" He shot his eyes over to me, but I couldn't decide what his expression meant. "So they're going to cooperate? They're taking the deal?"

My lungs got so tight I felt as if they were going to completely close themselves off from the rest of my body, but I didn't say a word. I couldn't. It would take too much air, and I didn't have a bit of it to spare.

"How soon?" he asked, reaching for my hand.

His felt warm and strong, a steady reassurance that

he would be by my side through whatever might come.

"And she doesn't have to be there?" Ethan asked, although it didn't come across as much of a question. "She doesn't have to face him yet?"

A few more moments passed by with nothing but the soft buzzing of the voice on the other end of the line being drowned out by Carter's laughter and Snoopy's energetic efforts to eat his frozen yogurt.

Finally, Ethan ended the call. "It's happening fast," he said.

"How fast?"

"Tomorrow. Both of the guys already agreed to take the deal. Lennon's going to be there. They'll arrest him and charge him on the spot, as soon as he steps into the courthouse."

"And he won't get a lesser sentence?" I asked, trying to keep my voice from cracking...but I failed. I failed miserably. And now, my eyes were welling with tears.

I wasn't sure why I was crying now. He couldn't hurt me anymore. He was finally going to pay for what he'd done, at least in some small way. Why should that make me cry? I ought to be happy. Or relieved. But instead, I felt overwhelmed.

"His lawyers might try to get a plea bargain of some sort, but if his buddies testify against him, and you and I testify against him, he won't get off." Ethan tossed his phone on the sofa and reached over to brush away my tears, which only caused more to fall. "You've got medical evidence to back you up. There's video showing what the other guys did to you. It'll be enough. It has to be."

I was glad Ethan seemed certain, because I

definitely didn't.

"And I don't have to be there? When they arrest him?" Because I didn't think I was ready for that yet. Yes, someday, I'd have to face him in a trial. But I needed time to prepare. I needed more time to heal.

"You don't have to be there. He's never going to be able to hurt you again, Nat. I'm going to make sure of it."

"So the only way he can keep hurting me now is if I let him," I said.

"Like if you don't let yourself love someone."

He didn't need to fill in the blanks any more than that. I knew Ethan meant I needed to allow myself to love him.

And I wanted to. I wanted to feel free enough to love him and Carter and Snoopy.

Someday.

I would get there.

I had to.

Chapter Thirty-Two

Ethan

I did my best to focus on the time I had with my son, on Natalie and everything she needed from me, and on hockey since it was my job, but there was no way I could begin to breathe easy again until I knew that Lennon had been arrested for all the shit he'd put Natalie through. Soon, they told us. They were working on it, but everything in the legal system takes time.

Our back-to-back games went relatively well. We came away with a checkmark in the W column against Winnipeg and a loss against Chicago. We might have had a better chance at beating Chicago if we'd faced them in the first game of the back-to-back weekend, but no one had consulted us as to our preference. This was our schedule, so we had to deal with it.

Carter couldn't stop chattering the whole way home from the game against the Blackhawks. "Did you *see* the way Toews went top-shelf?"

"I saw it," I drawled. "I saw it better than you did since I was the guy who couldn't tie up the guy's stick in time."

"He's too good for you, Dad."

And my kid was too smart for his own good—and for my pride. Ouch. "He got the better of me this time. Might not be the case next time." It would've helped if Viktor Frisk had tracked back into our defensive zone better. He'd lost his man, and in the process, he'd left me and Prince out to dry. Hunter had just about lost his shit on Frisky, and I couldn't say I blamed him. We could've beaten those guys if not for a handful of careless mistakes like that one.

Carter kept yammering on and on in the back seat the rest of the way home, and Natalie and I let him. Kids tended to get worked up from all the adrenaline at an event like that.

Or at least my kid did. Maybe others weren't as susceptible to the big high followed by the huge drop of energy. He would wear himself out before too much longer, and then he'd probably crash hard— which would give me and Natalie some time to talk, just the two of us.

He was still blabbering about the game when I pulled into the garage. As soon as I'd put the car in park, he barreled out of his seat and raced inside to get some puppy love.

"They should both sleep hard tonight," Natalie said softly.

"Good. His mom prefers for me to send him home well rested before school. He doesn't get as many red cards if he's had enough sleep."

She laughed—an amazing sound to my ears—and reached simultaneously for her purse and the door handle to get out of the car.

The garage door started to close behind us, but

then I caught a glimpse of something in my rearview mirror that chilled my blood.

My father.

He was standing in my driveway, arms crossed. It was the same stance he'd always taken up just before beating the snot out of me.

Natalie glanced over at me, and her easy smile quickly dissipated, fizzling like fireworks falling out of the sky. "What? Is Hayes here?" Her voice rose to a high-pitched squeak of fear that gnawed at me from the inside out. She turned to look behind us, but the garage door blocked her view, which only ramped up her tension to a higher degree.

"It's not Hayes," I said. "I need you to go inside and stay with Carter and Snoopy."

Everything flooded out of her in a rush. "You can't fight with Hayes again. You really can't. You can't hit him. It's a trap. He's trying to get you to beat him up so he can press charges against you, or so he can use it in court to prove that we're in a relationship or something, that you were—"

"It's *not Hayes*," I repeated more firmly, but the terror in her expression nearly ripped my guts out through my throat. But she still wouldn't budge. "It's my father," I explained, hoping that would be enough to get her moving.

"Your…" Her voice trailed off as understanding dawned in her eyes. "I'm coming with you."

"I want you to go inside."

"You might need a witness. I can have my phone ready to call 9-1-1. I can film a video. You might need evidence."

"Please, Nat." I took both of her hands in my own and squeezed hard enough to catch her attention and force her to meet my eyes. "I need you to go inside with Carter. Do it for me, okay? If anything happens, I need you to be there for my kid. And Snoopy can help protect both of you."

I didn't like having to put the situation into such stark terms, but she'd been through enough to understand the reality of the situation.

And reality was looking really fucking grim right now.

Her chin and lips trembled, and it seemed as if she was bound to start crying at any moment. But then she squared her shoulders and gave me a curt nod. "But I'm going to be watching out the window. I'll be ready to call for help."

"With any luck, you won't need to."

"If luck exists, we should be due some by now." She almost smiled, too. "I'm filming it, too. Just in case."

"That's my girl." I bent closer for a quick, hard kiss. She hesitated for just a moment, clinging to me like her life depended on it, but then she took her purse and headed for the kitchen door to be with my kid and his dog, finding a new level of strength that she might not have realized she possessed.

I'd known it, though. I realized it all the way back when she was unconscious in the hospital. Hell, I probably knew it even before then. Natalie was a hell of a lot stronger than she ever gave herself credit for.

"Tell Carter he needs to take a bath, okay?" I called after her. "Then he'll be distracted." And maybe it would be enough to distract her, too.

She met my eyes and held them for a moment before disappearing inside my house.

I headed out the man door and found my father in

exactly the same position I'd last seen him. "Something I can do for you?" I ground out.

He actually smirked at me, the son of a bitch. "Your girl's pretty. No wonder you wanted to get with her. I bet she's got a nice, tight pussy for you, too. I wouldn't mind having a bit of that, myself."

"If you don't have anything better than that to say to me, you can get the fuck off my property before I call the police and have you escorted off it."

"You don't wanna do that, now, son."

"The hell I don't. I'd love to see you hauled off in the back of a police cruiser with your hands cuffed behind you."

He shook his head, looking smug. "No, promise. You don't want to do that. Not if you want things to go in your favor when it comes to her ex."

"The fuck are you talking about?" I demanded.

"Brought your mother down with me this time."

My hand curled into a fist, as if of its own volition. "Where is she?"

"You haven't seen her in a long time," he continued, going on at his own pace and completely ignoring my question. "Too long. Your mother misses you. You took off and left us behind, and you broke her heart."

"If anyone broke her heart, it's you—her heart and just about every other part of her."

"You can think what you want, Ethan, but nothing hurt her worse than you walking out and leaving us behind, closing us out of your life. Shutting us out of your kid's life. I saw him last week. Did you know that? Found out what school his mother has him in and went by there. He's really good at getting across the monkey bars. No big surprise. He's got your arms—just like a fucking monkey's arms."

Before I realized what I was doing, I'd closed the distance between us and was half a breath away from closing my hand around his throat and shutting off his windpipe.

"You don't like that, do you, son?" my father said, laughing.

The son of a bitch was fucking laughing.

"Don't call me son."

"You are my son."

"But you're not a very good father. Never have been."

"Doesn't change the truth. You think you're a good father? You think there's such a thing as a good father in this world?"

"You go near my kid again, and I'll have you behind bars before you can blink."

"You won't know," he shot back. "You'll be down here, chasing your big-dollar contracts and some pussy that rightfully belongs to one of your teammates, and you won't be able to do a goddamned thing about it. Besides, you'd be too fucking scared of the consequences."

"You're the one who's scared. You've been scared of me ever since I got to be bigger than you. That's why you've got to play this game now."

"No one's playing games here but you, son."

"This has never been a game. This is someone's fucking life you're messing with. Several lives, actually. And I'm not going to let you get away with it anymore."

"You always talked a big game, especially when it came to your mother. Said you were going to get away from me and take her with you, but you never followed through."

He was trying to bait me. I knew it, and I knew better than to fall prey to it, but damn if I didn't want to rip his throat out. "I tried to follow through."

"Tried and failed. And you never did stop to think about the consequences of your actions, did you?"

He wanted to talk about fucking *consequences*? Who the fuck did he think needed to face up to some goddamned consequences?

Breathe. I had to calm down before I let him goad me into doing something stupid.

"This isn't about my mother," I ground out.

He was trying to distract me, and it was working. I couldn't let him do that. I still hadn't figured out what his game was this time, other than possibly attempting to tempt me into taking a swing at him. Maybe he had a camera somewhere, ready to catch me going for him. Maybe he was going to try to use that to work against me in court and aid Lennon's case.

I couldn't let that happen. I had to keep my cool.

"It's not about Mom, and it's not about Natalie," I said, choosing my words carefully, "and it damned sure isn't about my son. This is about you and me. This is about right here and right now."

"Ethan?" a small voice implored from across the street.

A small *female* voice.

And it was entirely too familiar, even if I hadn't heard her for years.

I took my gaze off my father for long enough to check out the black sedan parked facing the wrong way on the street behind him. The front passenger-side window was rolled down far enough for me to make out a head of dark, curly hair tinged with gray.

In the time it took me to glance over, my father's expression went from spiteful to downright mean. "The fuck did I tell you, Lydia?"

He took off toward the car with a familiar, purposeful stride—the one that said I was about to get the ever-loving shit kicked out of me. But he was going for my mother, not for me.

I didn't stop to think. Didn't have it in me. The son of a bitch was about to beat my mother.

I took off after him.

Consequences?

Fuck consequences.

Chapter Thirty-Three

Natalie

"Don't you dare step one foot outside and get involved in this," London snarled at me into the speakerphone. "If you do, I will personally ride over your bad leg with my wheelchair a few dozen times, you got that? Dima and Razor are both on their way, and so are the police. And they've probably got a few more of the guys coming by now, too. But you and Carter are staying put inside that house, or I swear to God, you won't want to face my wrath."

I peeked through the mini-blinds again, Carter and Snoopy at my side, both as anxious as I was. "But how can I help him if I'm in here?"

"He wants you inside where you're safe, dummy."

"I know." I groaned. "I'm staying put. But I feel like I should be doing *something*."

"Can you record what's happening?"

"Not while I'm on the phone with you."

"Well, let's hang up then," she replied. "Better to have evidence."

"But what if—"

"My iPad!" Carter shouted.

"Good idea," London replied. "Go get it, buddy. Hurry. Go fast."

He looked at me for approval. I gave him a quick nod, and he took off up the stairs to dig through his backpack.

For once, Snoopy didn't tail his boy, but instead stayed right by my side. His attention was trained fully on Ethan and Ethan's father, just like mine. That dog didn't move a muscle, and his ears and tail were on high alert, a low, menacing growl rumbling through his chest.

Ethan had his hand on his father's throat. A shudder coursed through me. It was so eerily similar to the night Hayes had attacked me in the parking lot, the way Ethan had tried to save me. But even though I knew his father deserved every bit of this and more because of all the things he'd done to Ethan, I also knew there had to be something else going on here. Something I couldn't see.

There *had* to be. Didn't there?

Ethan wouldn't do something like this without good reason—especially not while Hayes's legal team was still attempting to use this very sort of behavior as a defense.

"I don't get it," I said to London. "I don't know why's Ethan's doing this. Why now? Why would he fall into that trap?"

"Everyone has a breaking point. Maybe his father knows what Ethan's is. Maybe he said something that caused Ethan to snap."

"Yeah. Maybe."

"If anyone would know his triggers, it'd be his father."

I didn't want to think about Ethan having triggers that would set him off like this. I didn't want to think about him snapping. Because what if I stayed with him? What if I set him off someday? Or what if Carter did, or even Snoopy? And if that happened, as horrible as the thought might be, could I leave? Could I walk away, knowing he might hurt his son if he didn't have me there to hurt instead? Could I leave knowing he might do something to harm that little boy?

A lead weight settled in my gut at the thought.

I couldn't go there. Not now.

The clatter of Carter's feet rushing back down the stairs was the only sound to disturb the painful tension. "Here, Natalie!" he said, thrusting his iPad into my hands.

Leaving the phone on speaker, I set it down on the window ledge and started filming through the blinds with the iPad. I zoomed in as close as I could without thoroughly compromising the quality of the video, staring at the screen in shock.

Because someone else was climbing out of the car.

"He brought someone else with him! Ethan can maybe hold off his father, but if they team up against—"

"You're not going out there," London shouted at me. "Don't even think about it."

"But if it's Hay—"

"If it's Hayes, then he's hoping you'll come out there. Don't be stupid. You're not going to be the dumb-ass blonde in the movie who thinks she can fend off men twice her size and ends up getting both herself and the badass hero in bigger trouble than they were in to start with."

Even though I knew she was right, I didn't want to acknowledge it. Didn't want to believe it. Didn't want it to be true.

"Who's that lady?" Carter asked.

A lady? I strained my eyes to see, but whoever had gotten out of the car was still obscured by Ethan and his father. But then Ethan shoved his father against the side of the car, and I realized Carter was right. It was a small woman with graying hair. And she was tugging on Ethan's arms, trying to get him to release his father.

"Carter, I need you to do me a favor," I said. "Can you open the window?" Maybe then we'd be able to hear what was going on without going outside.

"Good plan," London said. "You'll probably have to flip the window locks open. Can you reach them?"

"I'll get a chair," he said. The next thing I knew, he was dragging a chair from the dining room into the living room. He climbed on top of it and stretched to open the locks, and moments later, he slid the window up.

"You have to let him go," the woman pleaded, still tugging on Ethan's arms. "Please. You can't kill him."

I zoomed in on her face, because something seemed off.

Bruises. Dark, purple bruises all over her face.

Ethan's mother. It had to be. I needed to get better images. Better sound. I couldn't do that from inside the house.

"Stay here," I said to Carter, and before he could stop me, I hurried out the front door, his iPad still filming, leaving my cell phone with him while Snoopy barked in my wake and London shouted something unintelligible at me.

Chapter Thirty-Four

Ethan

The bastard wouldn't stop squirming.

Somehow, he broke my grip for long enough that he could take a swing at me, but he missed me and got Mom, instead.

Or maybe that was what he'd intended to begin with. Wouldn't surprise me.

Mom didn't even make a sound, even though he'd pelted her hard enough that she crumpled to the ground at my feet before I got him back under my control, my thumbs pressing on his windpipe.

"You fucking bastard," I said.

He laughed. It made me want to end him right now. I could do it. It'd be easy. A bit more pressure, and his life would be over.

"You think this is funny?"

He couldn't speak, but his eyes shifted to somewhere behind me.

I took one quick glance over my shoulder and immediately wished I hadn't, because Natalie was racing toward us. "What the hell are you doing out here?" I demanded. "Go back inside. For all we know, Hayes is on his way here. Please, Nat."

But she didn't respond to me. I might as well have been invisible to her. She kept coming and didn't stop until she was at my mother's side.

She got down on the ground next to Mom. Only then did I realize she had something in her hands, because she had to set it down in order to help make my mother more comfortable.

"I've got you. Help's on the way. You're going to be all right," Natalie said. "Ethan and I are going to make sure of it, okay?"

Then she shifted things around, and I was able to see what it was she'd brought out with her—Carter's iPad.

Fucking brilliant. Maybe she shouldn't be out here at all, but at least she was being smart enough to gather evidence.

Once she had some cloth covering the gash my father had opened up on Mom's cheek, she picked the iPad up again, moving it so she could capture all the visible wounds on my mother before turning it back to the two of us.

"Tell us what's going on, Ethan," she said, calmer and more in control than I'd ever known her to be. It made my chest full to bursting with pride, but there wasn't time for that now.

I took a quick glance back at her to be sure she had the camera on me now. Then I squeezed my father's windpipe harder, making sure he couldn't make a sound. "My bastard father's been beating the shit out of my mother. He's been doing it for years. Decades. He used to beat me up, too, until I got big enough to fight back. Now he's trying to tell the world that I'm full of shit. He wants to discredit me as a witness, saying that I've been making up stories my whole life about how he beat me and my mom up, and now I'm spreading lies about Hayes Lennon beating you up. Well, here's the evidence of what he's done to my mother."

Mom whimpered, but she didn't try to deny it. Thank fuck for that. Maybe this could all work out for the best in the end. Maybe this would be the final straw, the way I could get her out of the shitty situation she'd been in since before I was born.

If this wasn't enough, if she hadn't reached the end of her rope yet...

I couldn't even think like that. It *had* to be enough.

"Mrs. Higgins," Natalie said, "we got video of your husband striking you just now. I just want you to know that."

"But it's..." Mom's voice shook so hard I could barely hear her. "It's no use."

"What's no use?" I demanded. "You don't have to go home with him. You can stay here with us. You don't *ever* have to go home with this son of a bitch again."

Before she could respond, two squad cars came around the corner, their lights flashing and sirens blaring. The officers got out of their cars with their weapons drawn, two from each vehicle.

"Hands in the air," one of them shouted at me.

"I'll put them in the air as soon as one of you restrains him," I bit off.

"We'll restrain you both at the same time," he shot back.

I nodded my agreement.

Two of the officers came forward to deal with breaking us apart. I waited until one of them had my father's hands in cuffs behind his back before willingly releasing him.

The other officer nodded for me to turn around.

"Am I under arrest?" I demanded.

"Not yet. Not until we have a better understanding of what's going on here. But since you were just choking this other man, I think we'll all feel safer if you're cuffed while we do this, all right?"

I met Natalie's eyes over his shoulder. They were full of fear. My father was spewing a litany of curses while the officer who'd cuffed him led him a few feet away from us, and another officer—a woman—bent to the ground next to Mom and Natalie.

I nodded my agreement. "Go on. Cuff me, but get someone to take care of my mom."

"We've got an ambulance on the way," he said, taking his cuffs out and moving behind me.

"You all right, ma'am?" the female officer asked Mom.

She started to nod, but then a sob tore free.

"We need to get her checked out at a hospital," Natalie insisted. She lifted a bloodied piece of cloth away from my mother's cheek. "This one's fresh, but it looks like she's probably got a lot more injuries."

"As soon as the ambulance arrives," the officer said.

Razor and Dima pulled up within moments of one another, both of them hurrying out of their cars to see what they could do. Dima went into the house to check on Carter and Snoopy, and they both ran back outside with him. Carter went right up to Natalie and sat on the street, crisscross-applesauce style, drawing Snoopy down to sit next to him.

"You okay, buddy?" I asked him.

He sniffled, but he nodded resolutely. "Why'd they put you in handcuffs? Are you gonna go to jail?"

"He's not going to jail," Natalie reassured him. And I hoped she was right, but it was a thin hope. I'd had my hands on my father's throat when they'd pulled up. Maybe it was in defense of my mother, but I'd still been strangling him.

Within minutes, the cops had everyone separated to be interviewed about what had happened. I kept an eye on Natalie, Carter, and my mom the whole time, patiently answering the officers' questions.

After twenty minutes or so, they'd stopped asking me questions for the time being and had me sitting on the curb, still cuffed. Dima and Razor both came over to sit next to me.

"Not looking good, man," Razor said.

"They'll arrest me," I replied. They had to.

"You'll get off, though."

"Maybe. Probably. But there'll have to be a trial."

"Fuck," Dima muttered.

That about summed it up.

I watched as the paramedics loaded my mother onto a gurney and lifted her into the back of the ambulance, despite her sobbing protests.

"I'll go," Dima said. "Calling London to come, too. She'll leave baby with Dana and Zee."

I nodded, because I was too choked up to say anything.

He got up and jumped into the back of the ambulance with the paramedics and my mother, his phone in his hand to make the call.

"This is going to be major news," Razor pointed out.

"I'm going to be suspended."

"Surely they won't—"

"Wanna bet?" I cut in. I cocked a brow at him. "When has anyone in the league been arrested for anything and not been suspended? At least temporarily."

"But they'll rescind it pretty fast. Once they can look at all the evidence..."

"It's not going to be fast."

He grunted. "Maybe not."

Then he looked over at Natalie, Carter, and Snoopy. My kid and his dog were sticking like glue to her side. They had to be scared out of their minds, but Carter was handling this better than a lot of grown men would.

"He flies home tomorrow?" Razor asked.

"Yeah."

"They can come home with one of us tonight. You know—if they have to keep you overnight or whatever. Whoever Natalie feels most comfortable with."

I nodded because I was too choked up to respond.

He pulled out his phone. "I'm calling Gary. The sooner he knows what's going on, the sooner he can work on getting you out."

Hell. I'd hardly thought about the team's response, let alone the league's. This was quickly becoming a much bigger nightmare than I'd ever anticipated.

And now I had to figure out how I was going to explain all of this to Kinsey, too.

Just when I most wished I could bury my head in the sand and never bring it out again, Natalie caught my eye. She tugged Carter onto her lap, and Snoopy rested his chin on top of my son's knees—and then Natalie gave me the smallest smile.

I'd gone and fucked up a lot of things in a single stupid move—but maybe not everything.

Chapter Thirty-Five

Natalie

In the end, the police arrested both Ethan and his father, and the paramedics took his mother to the hospital to be evaluated, and I was left behind with Carter and Snoopy. Dima went to the hospital with Ethan's mother, and Razor stayed behind with me, helping me sort out how I could get Carter to the airport tomorrow if Ethan wasn't released in time to do it.

That turned out not to be necessary—a couple of the higher-ups involved with the team managed to press the courts to set bail in a timely fashion, and he easily met it. They had already set things in motion for the league to determine what sort of repercussions he might have to face—a fine or a suspension, most likely, but we would have to wait to see how the league ruled. Still, by lunchtime the day after all the drama, Ethan was home.

The same could not be said for either of his parents. The bail set for his father was more than the elder Higgins could post as of yet, and the doctors decided to keep Mrs. Higgins in the hospital overnight for observation, as she had a broken orbital bone, and they were concerned about a possible concussion.

"Dad!" Carter rushed to his father's side the moment he came through the door.

I wasn't far behind him, but I was too overcome with emotion to say a word.

Ethan wrapped his strong arms around both of us, lifting us off the floor in an enormous bear hug. I sobbed against his shoulder, holding on for all I was worth.

"That was the longest night I've ever had," I said when he finally set me back on my feet.

He kissed me hard. "Not for me."

"No?"

"No. The first night you were in the hospital. Hell, all the nights you were in the hospital, but especially the ones when you were unconscious. They were a lot longer."

For some reason, that simple statement made my stomach flutter.

I blinked back tears and stepped away, wanting to give Ethan some time with his son. They needed it after the drama and trauma of yesterday.

He didn't let me get too far, though. He snagged me around the waist and tugged me onto his lap on the couch. Carter jumped up beside him, and Snoopy followed suit, and Ethan tucked my head against his chest.

I felt so safe like that—safer than I'd allowed myself to feel in years.

"Tomorrow's the big day," Ethan said into the silence.

"Big day?" I repeated. I couldn't come up with what could be bigger than the last twenty-four hours or so.

"When they're going to arrest Lennon."

My heart pounded wildly against my ribs.

"And now that my father's facing charges, too, that's going to seriously hurt his defense," Ethan said. "He's not going to get away with it. Neither of them is going to get away with it."

I squeezed my eyes to keep my tears at bay, nodding slightly.

"How would you two feel about me asking my mom to come and live with us?" he asked.

I looked up at him in surprise.

Ethan shrugged. "She's going to need some support. Someone she can count on. This isn't going to be easy for her. She's been living like that for thirty-five years."

"So I can get to know my grandma?" Carter asked.

"If she wants to come, yeah." Ethan looked down into my eyes. "If you're okay with that. I mean, we've got that room all set up. She could have it. You won't be needing it anymore."

"I won't?" My breath fluttered through my lips.

"Not if you move up into my room with me." His face was a mixture of torture and hope. "I know you're not sure if you love me yet—"

"I do," I cut in, and this time, there were no tears. "I love you. I realized that in the middle of everything. Or—well, maybe I already knew it, but I *accepted* it then."

Ethan didn't immediately respond, but his expression was everything. Heat and love and fear, and maybe a bit of pride, all rolled up into one longing look. But then he turned to Carter. "You be okay with that? If we invite my mom to come live downstairs in Miss Natalie's room, and Natalie comes to stay with me?"

"Natalie could share my room," Carter said. "Snoopy wouldn't mind."

Ethan and I both burst out laughing.

"That's a sweet offer, buddy, but I think your room's going to get a little crowded. Your dog already takes up a lot of space, and you're growing like a weed."

Carter shrugged. "It's okay. I just want Natalie to stay. She can share your room."

"And you don't mind if we invite my mom to stay here, too?"

"She can't go back home with that man," Carter said adamantly.

"No. That's the plan."

He nodded. "She should stay here."

"Yeah?" Ethan asked, looking at his son.

"Yep."

"Yes," I agreed, too.

"Good," Ethan said. "You'd be okay if this became a permanent thing? All of us living here together?"

"Can we bring Mom, too?"

Ethan chuckled. "Your mom wants to stay in Michigan. Her parents are there."

"Yeah, I know."

"She's going to bring you down to visit for Thanksgiving, though."

"She's coming, too?" Carter said.

I nodded. "That's the plan." And my stomach clenched again at the thought, because it felt as if I would be put on trial. I knew I was overreacting with that, but I couldn't stop the sensation from creeping up on me.

"That's okay then. We should have my grandma come stay here."

Snoopy barked, as if to give his own consent.

Life was suddenly looking very different.

......

With Ethan's father in jail pending trial for domestic violence, and Alex and Jason agreeing to rat Hayes out in exchange for a lesser sentence, suddenly, the case against my ex was taking shape.

The day that they called to let me know the plan had worked—that Hayes had shown up in court to be sure his buddies didn't implicate him and he'd been arrested—was the first time in recent memory that I could take a full breath.

"It'll all be over soon," Ethan said over a glass of wine.

"I don't know about *soon*," I said.

"Soon is relative."

He was right about that.

His mother agreed to move in with us, although she required a lot of convincing. To be honest, she and Ethan didn't really know each other anymore. But in some ways, the three of us understood one another better than anyone else possibly could. We didn't even need to speak to know what the others were thinking and feeling a lot of times.

Once she recovered relatively well from her injuries, I started taking her with me to the group therapy sessions I still attended.

She didn't speak much—but she listened a lot. Listening was an excellent place to start. It could help her to understand that she wasn't alone, not even when she felt more alone than she'd ever felt before in her life.

"How can you let my son touch you?" she asked me one evening over dinner. The team was on the road, so it was just the two of us at Ethan's house. "After all the things *he* did to you, how can you let any man touch you?"

The way she'd emphasized *he* left no doubt who she meant.

"I couldn't let *any* man touch me," I said, carefully weighing my words. "Ethan's different."

"Different how?"

He was different in almost every way imaginable. But I said, "He's different because he loves me. Anyone who could hurt me the way Hayes did, anyone who could do the things to you that your husband did—they didn't love us."

She blinked, but it didn't stop fat tears from filling her eyes and spilling onto the table. "I don't know if I could allow that. I don't know if I could let a man love me."

And I nodded, and I reached across the table to squeeze her hand.

Because I knew.

I understood.

But there was nothing I could say that could make it better for her. I couldn't tell her that one day, she'd find the right man, and she'd be able to open up her heart and trust him enough to let him touch her.

Only she could know that for certain. And it might be a very long time before she'd be ready. It would probably be even longer before she'd believe it.

These things take time.

......

Kinsey and Carter came to baggage claim together, hand in hand—but the second Carter saw us, he dropped everything so he could race over to meet us.

But it wasn't his father's arms he jumped into. It wasn't his grandmother's arms, either.

He jumped into mine.

I was so surprised that I staggered under the impact, but Ethan put a hand behind my waist and steadied me. I wrapped my arms tight around him and didn't let go until he did.

"My mama wants to meet you," he finally said, backing away but holding tight to my hand.

Kinsey held out a hand to me with a warm smile that lit up her entire face. She and Carter had the same smile. It was easy to see how Carter was growing up to be such a sweet boy. With a father like Ethan and a mother who was obviously an equally good person, he'd have no choice but to be an amazing young man.

"Hi," I said, awkwardly reaching to shake her hand.

She drew me in for a hug, though.

"Oh… I…" didn't have the first clue how to respond.

"Welcome to the family," she said when she released me from her grip.

That was about all it took to cause fresh tears to sprout up.

She hugged Ethan's mother next, which caused the older woman to break down even worse than I had.

"It's been a long time," Kinsey said.

"Too long," Mrs. Higgins agreed, her sniffles

making it difficult to get the few words out.

"Why's everyone cryin'?" Carter asked.

I dug a pack of tissues out of my purse and passed them around. "We're just being silly," I said.

"We should get ice cream. Ice cream makes everything better. And when we go home, you should cuddle with Snoopy for a while."

I laughed and took Ethan's hand for the walk out to the car. Only a few months ago, I never would have imagined I'd believe that some ice cream and cuddling with a dog could make everything better. But now? Now I was starting to believe.

Roster

Name	Position	Nickname	Number
Travis Royal	Defense	Prince	2
Andrew Jensen	Defense	Jens	4
Vyacheslav Zherdev	Defense	Slava	5
Ray Chambers	Defense	Razor	6
Ethan Higgins	Defense	Huggy Bear	7
Alexei Petrov	Center	Petro	8
Eric Zellinger	Center	Zee	9
Sam Winchester	Right Wing	Sammy	10
Dmitri Nazarenko	Left Wing	Dima	14
Isaac Johnson	Defense	Ike	16
Ludvig Andersson	Left Wing	Luddy	17
Chris Richards	Center	Richie	18
Hayes Lennon'	Left Wing	Haymaker	19
Tom Kelly	Left Wing	Tommy Boy	22
Greg Bradshaw	Right Wing	Brady Bunch	23
Victor Frisk	Center	Frisky	27
Nathan Cochran	Defense	Nate	28
Hunter Fielding	Goal	Hunter	31
Shawn Hudson	Goal	Huds	33
Jacob Dresden	Right Wing	Jake	41
Andrew Nash	Right Wing	Drew	81
Seth McCormick	Right Wing	Mac	93

Books by Catherine Gayle

Contempory Romance

Breakaway
On the Fly
Taking a Shot
Light the Lamp
Delay of Game
Double Major
In the Zone
Holiday Hat Trick
Comeback
Dropping Gloves
Bury the Hatchet
Home Ice
Smoke Signals
Mistletoe Misconduct
Losing an Edge
Ghost Dance
Dreaming Up a Dare
Game Breaker
Rites of Passage
Defensive Zone
Power Play
Rain Dance

Historical Romance:

Twice a Rake
Saving Grace
Merely a Miss
Wallflower
Pariah
Seven Minutes in Devon
The Devil to Pay
A Dance with the Devil
An Unintended Journey
To Enchant an Icy Earl
Flight of Fancy
Rhyme and Reason
Thick as Thieves
Wanton Wives

Coming Soon:

Neutral Zone
Free Agent
Dream Catcher
Journeyman

About the Author

Catherine Gayle is a USA Today bestselling author of Regency-set historical romance and contemporary hockey romance. She's a transplanted Texan living in North Carolina with two extremely spoiled felines. In her spare time, she watches way too much hockey and reality TV, plans fun things to do for the Nephew Monster's next visit, and performs experiments in the kitchen which are rarely toxic.

www.ingramcontent.com/pod-product-compliance
Lightning Source LLC
Chambersburg PA
CBHW070658180626
46817CB00006B/2423